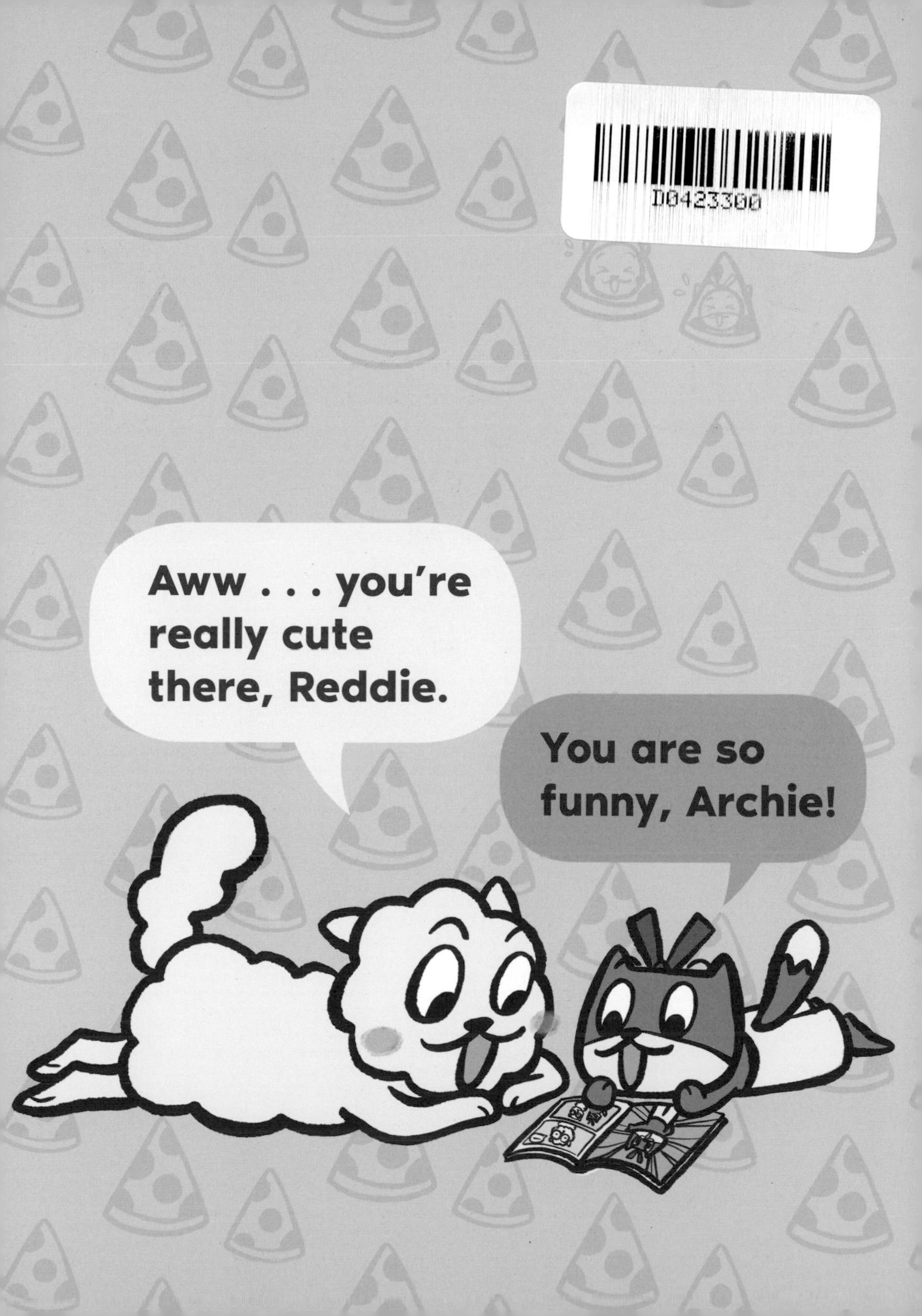
Aww . . . you're really cute there, Reddie.
You are so funny, Archie!

For Poppy Periwinkle.
We're nothing without you!

Special thanks to
Gemma Cooper and
Chris Hernandez.

RAZORBILL

An imprint of Penguin Random House LLC, New York

First published in the United States of America by Razorbill, an imprint of Penguin Random House LLC, 2021

Copyright © 2021 by Candy Robertson and Nicholas James Robertson

Visit us online at penguinrandomhouse.com.

Library of Congress Cataloging-in-Publication Data
Names: Robertson, Nicholas James, author. | Robertson, Candy, illustrator.
Title: I really dig pizza! : a mystery! / pictures and words by Candy James.
Description: New York : Razorbill, 2021. | Series: An Archie & Reddie book ; [1] | Audience: Ages 4–8. |
Summary: Archie the fox stumbles upon a cheesy treat in the forest and tries to keep it a secret, until his cousin Reddie comes along, ready to solve a mystery. Identifiers: LCCN 2021000851 |
ISBN 9780593350102 (hardcover) | ISBN 9780593350119 (ebook) | ISBN 9780593350126 (ebook)
Subjects: LCSH: Graphic novels. | CYAC: Graphic novels. | Friendship—Fiction. | Foxes—Fiction. |
Cousins—Fiction. | Pizza—Fiction. | Mystery and detective stories. | Humorous stories.
Classification: LCC PZ7.7.R6328 Iar 2021 | DDC 741.5952—dc23
LC record available at https://lccn.loc.gov/2021000851

Manufactured in China

1 3 5 7 9 10 8 6 4 2

Book design by Candy James. Text set in Noir Pro.

AN **ARCHiE & REDDiE** BOOK

I REALLY DIG PIZZA!

A MYSTERY!

PICTURES AND WORDS BY
CANDY JAMES

RAZORBILL

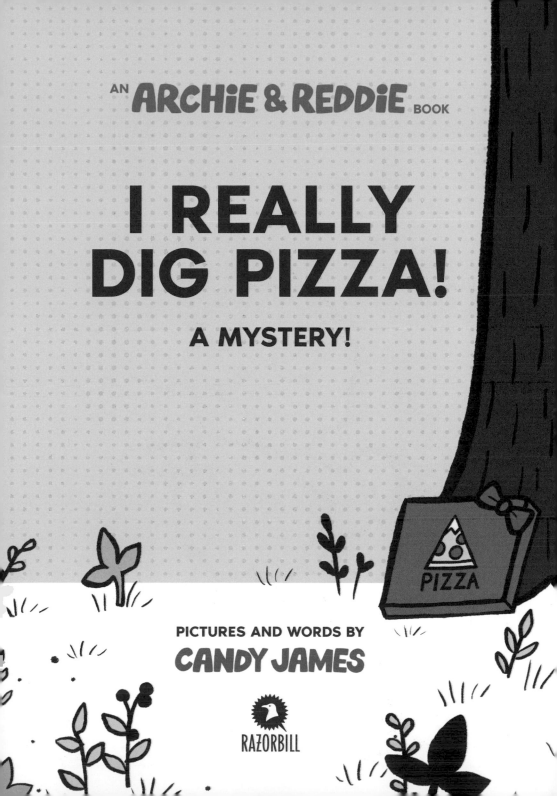

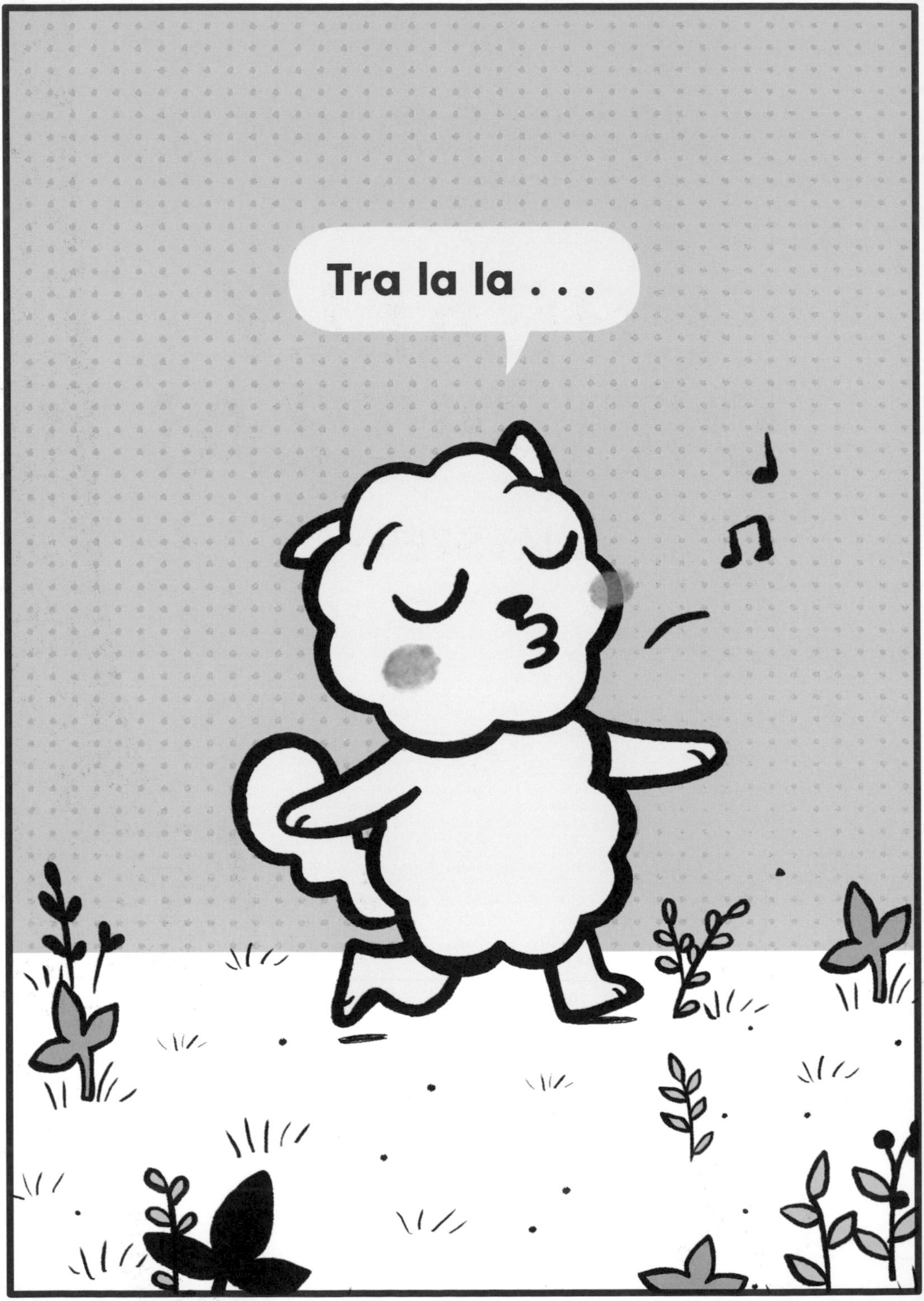
Tra la la . . .

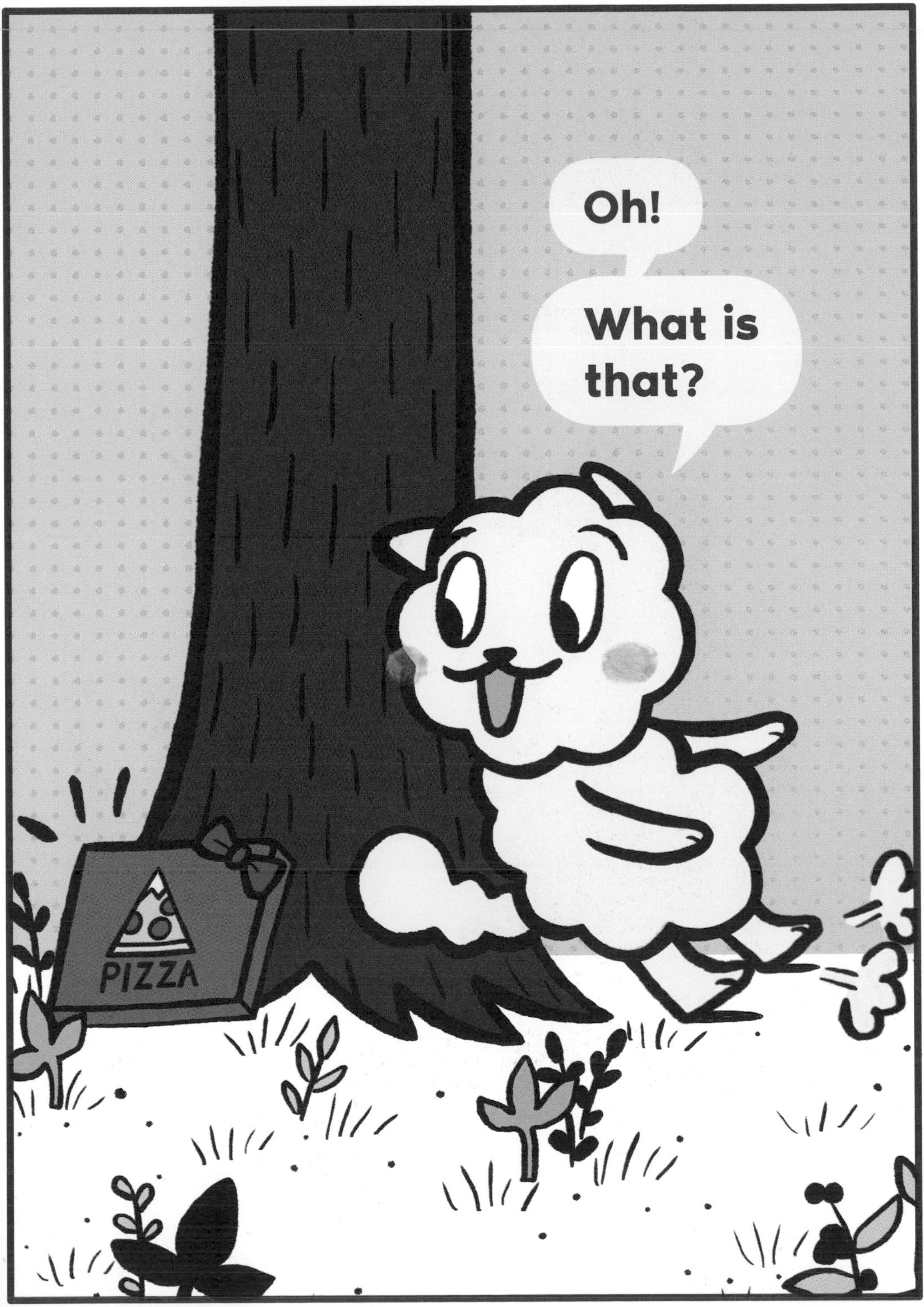
Oh!
What is that?
PIZZA

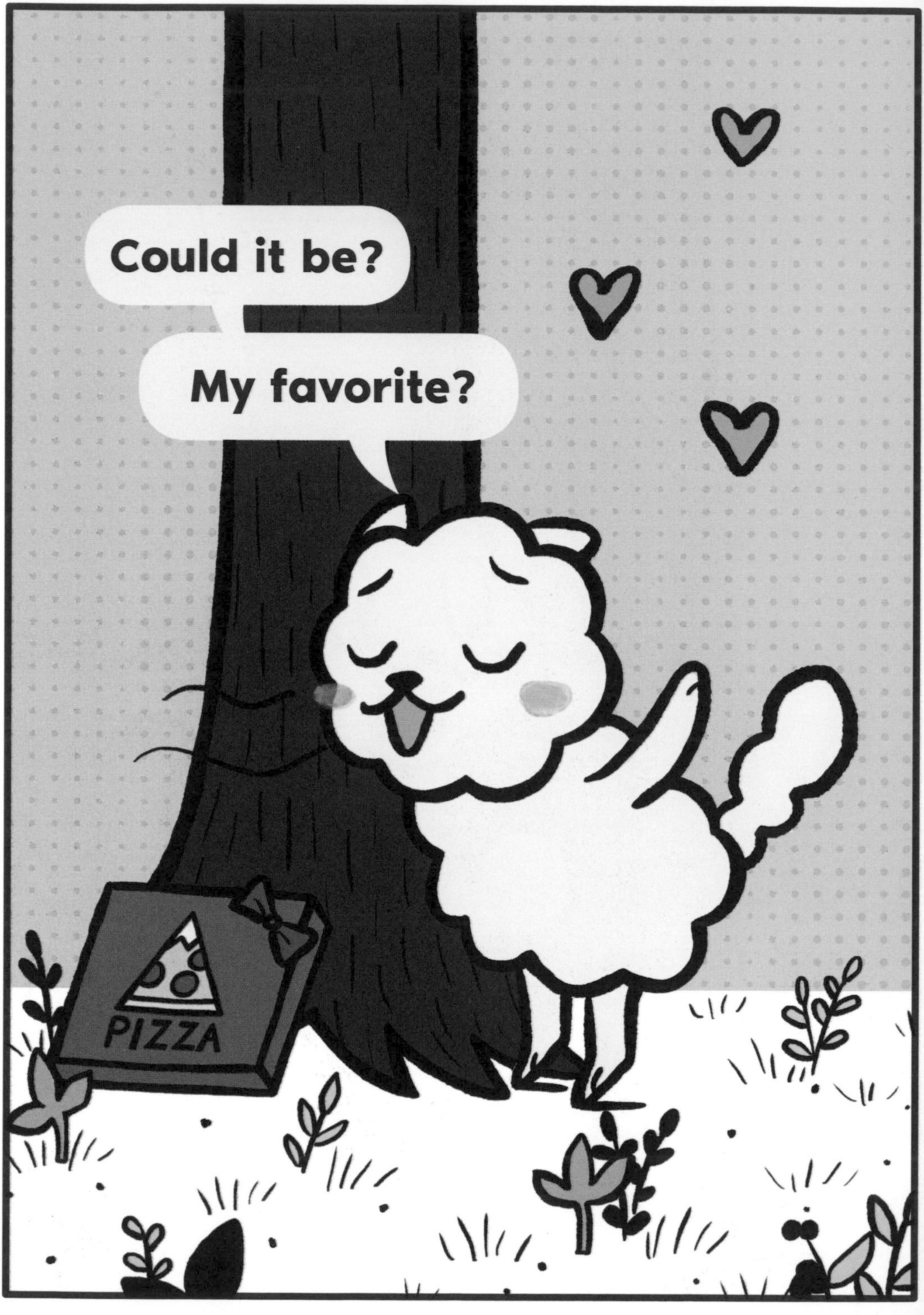
Could it be?
My favorite?
PIZZA

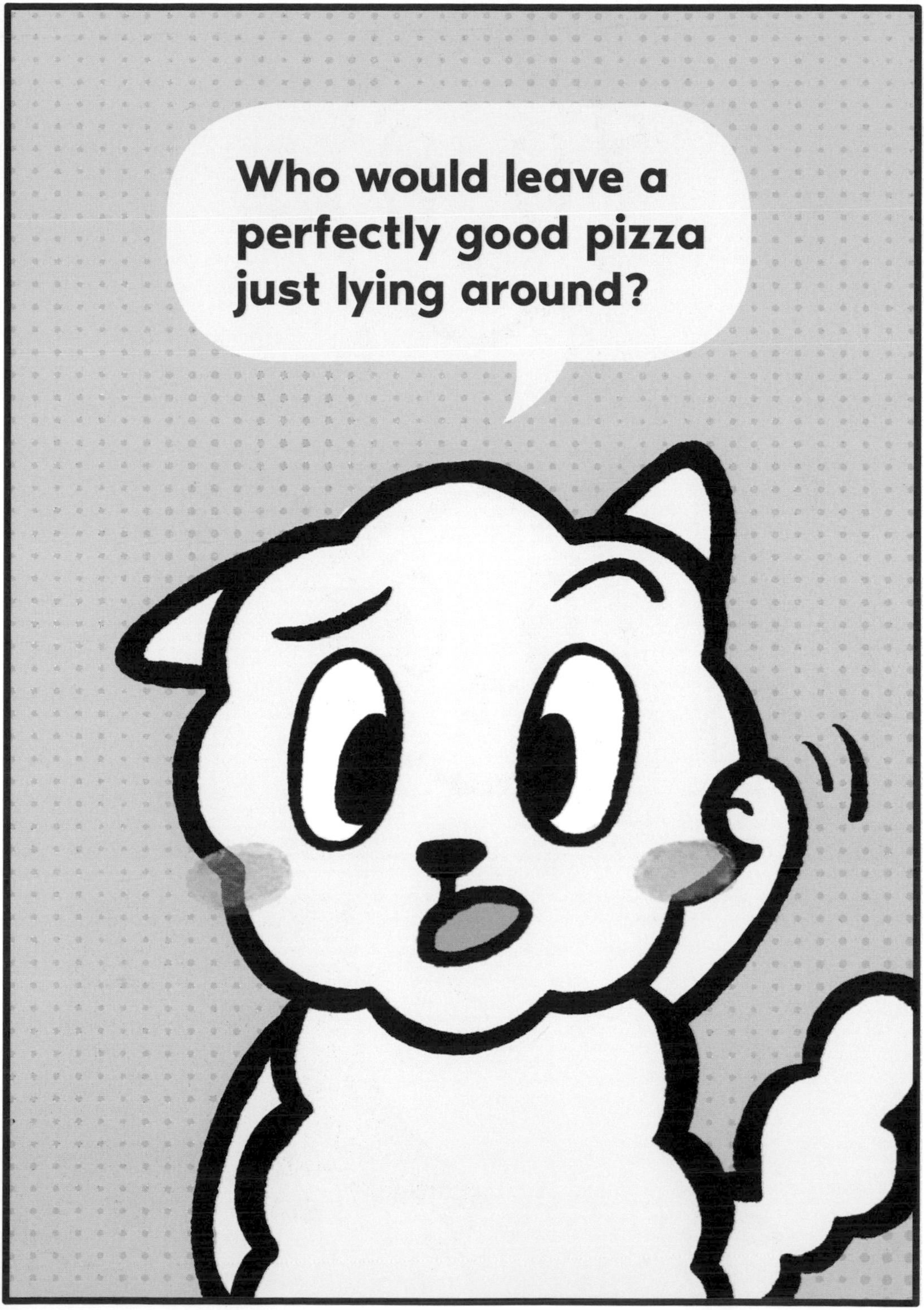
Who would leave a perfectly good pizza just lying around?

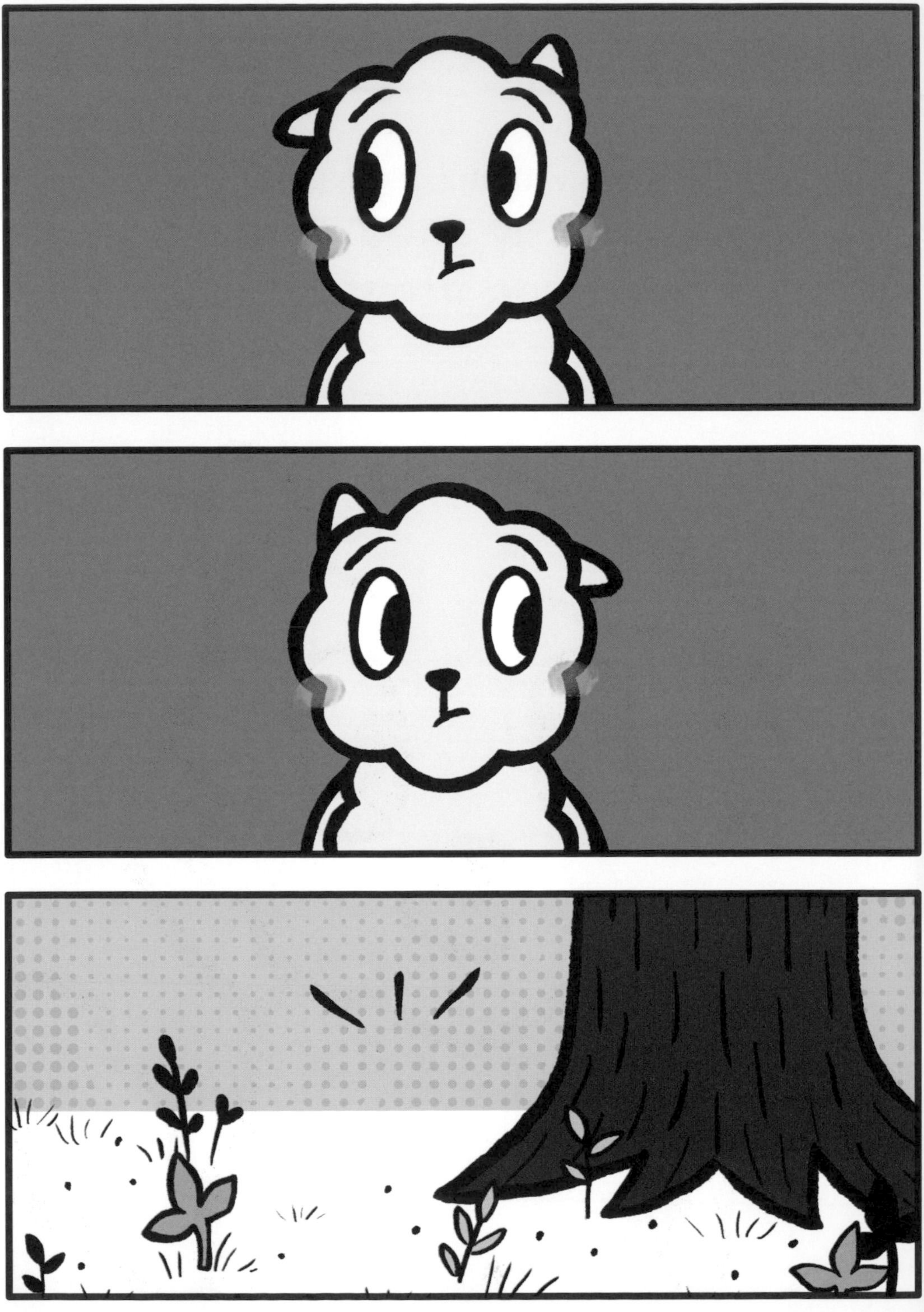

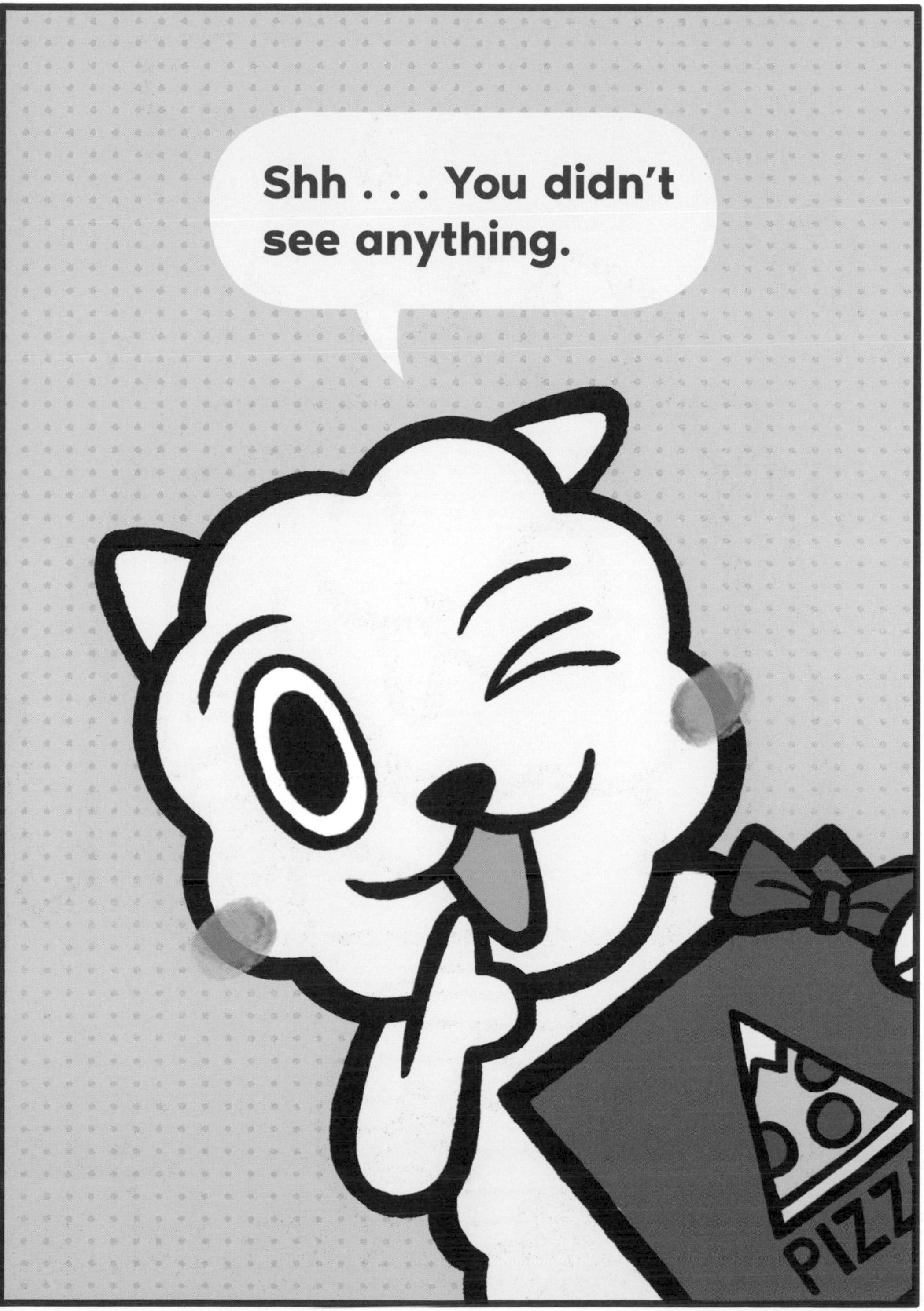
Shh . . . You didn't see anything.
PIZZ

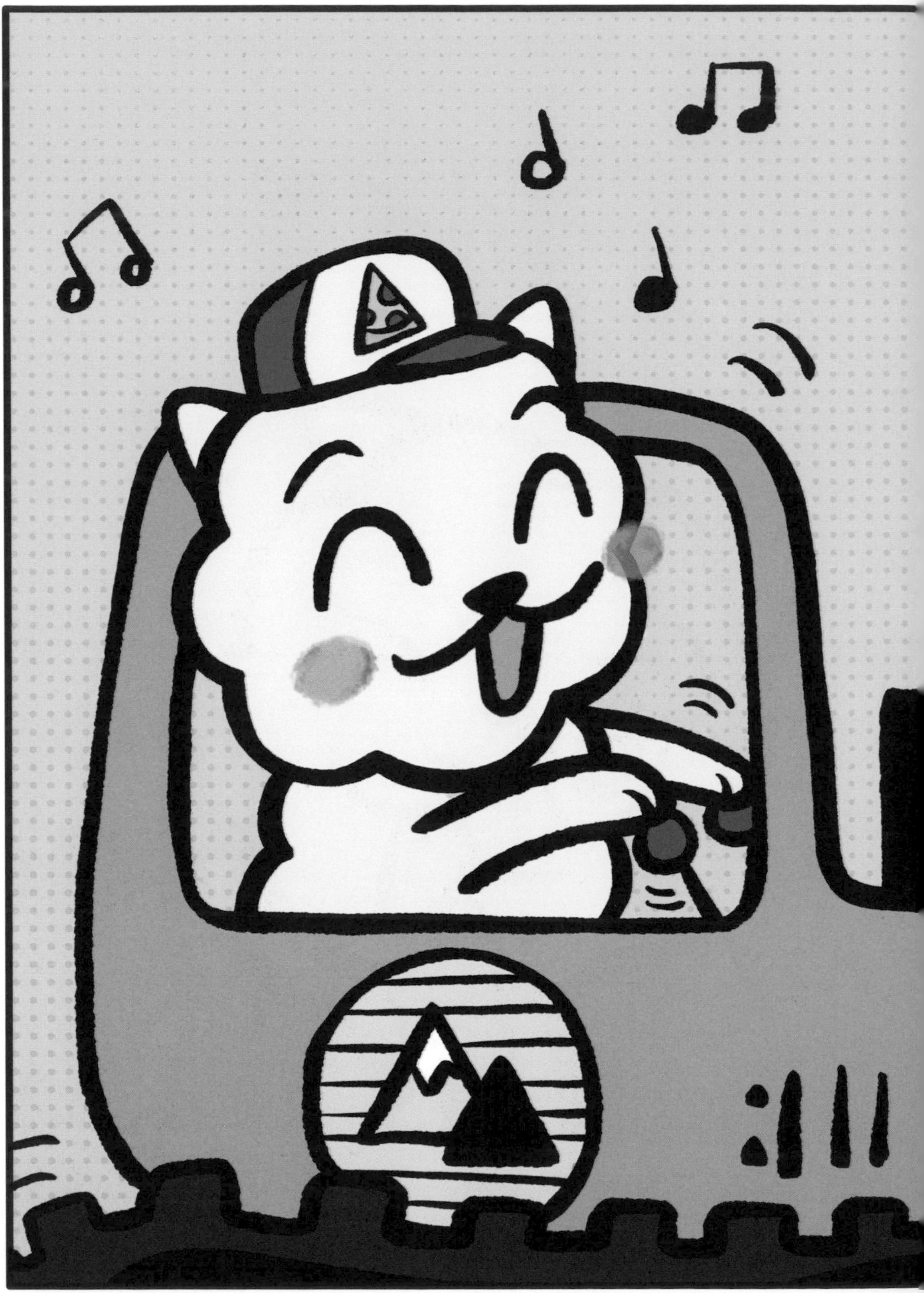

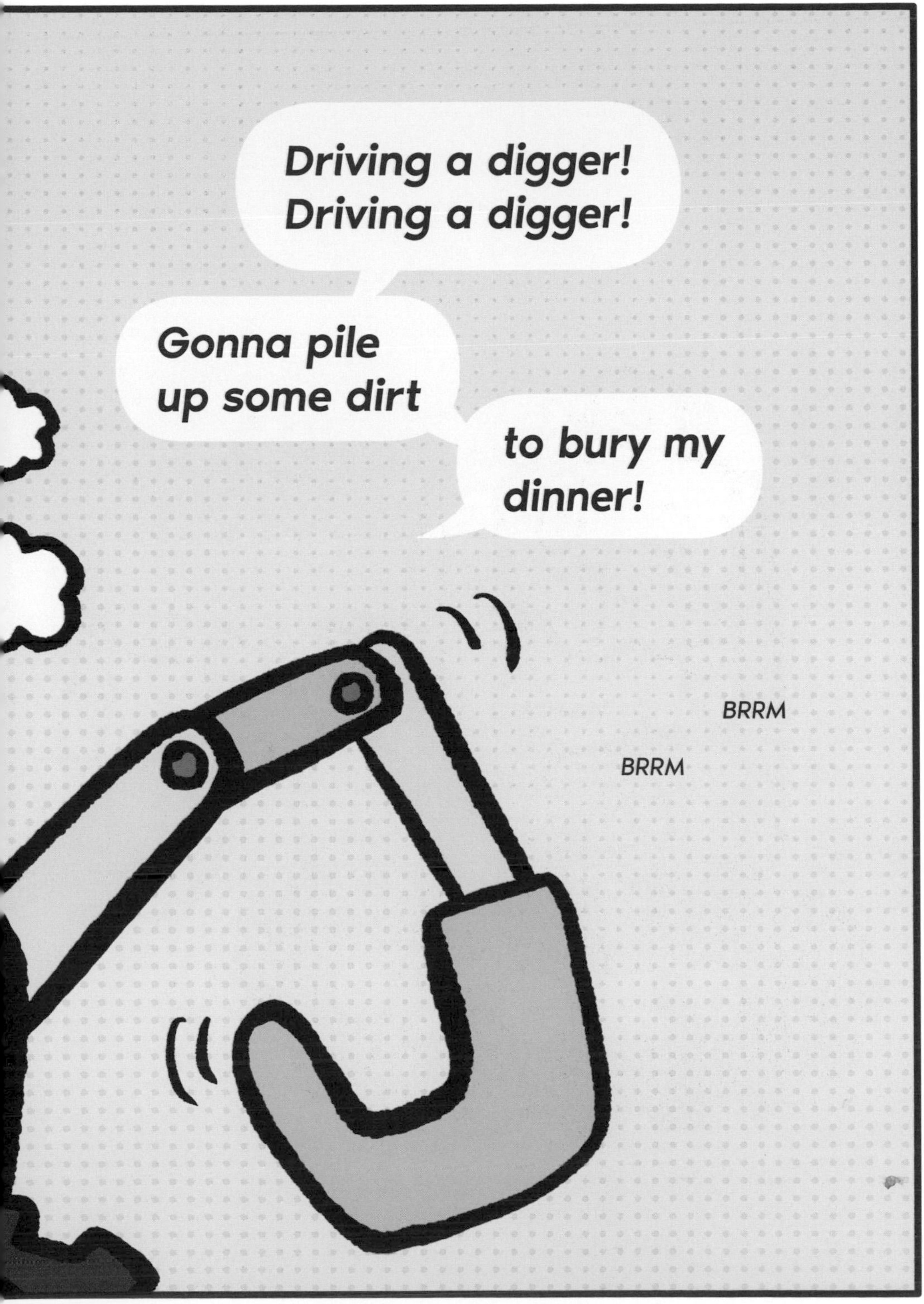
Driving a digger! Driving a digger!
Gonna pile up some dirt
to bury my dinner!
BRRM
BRRM

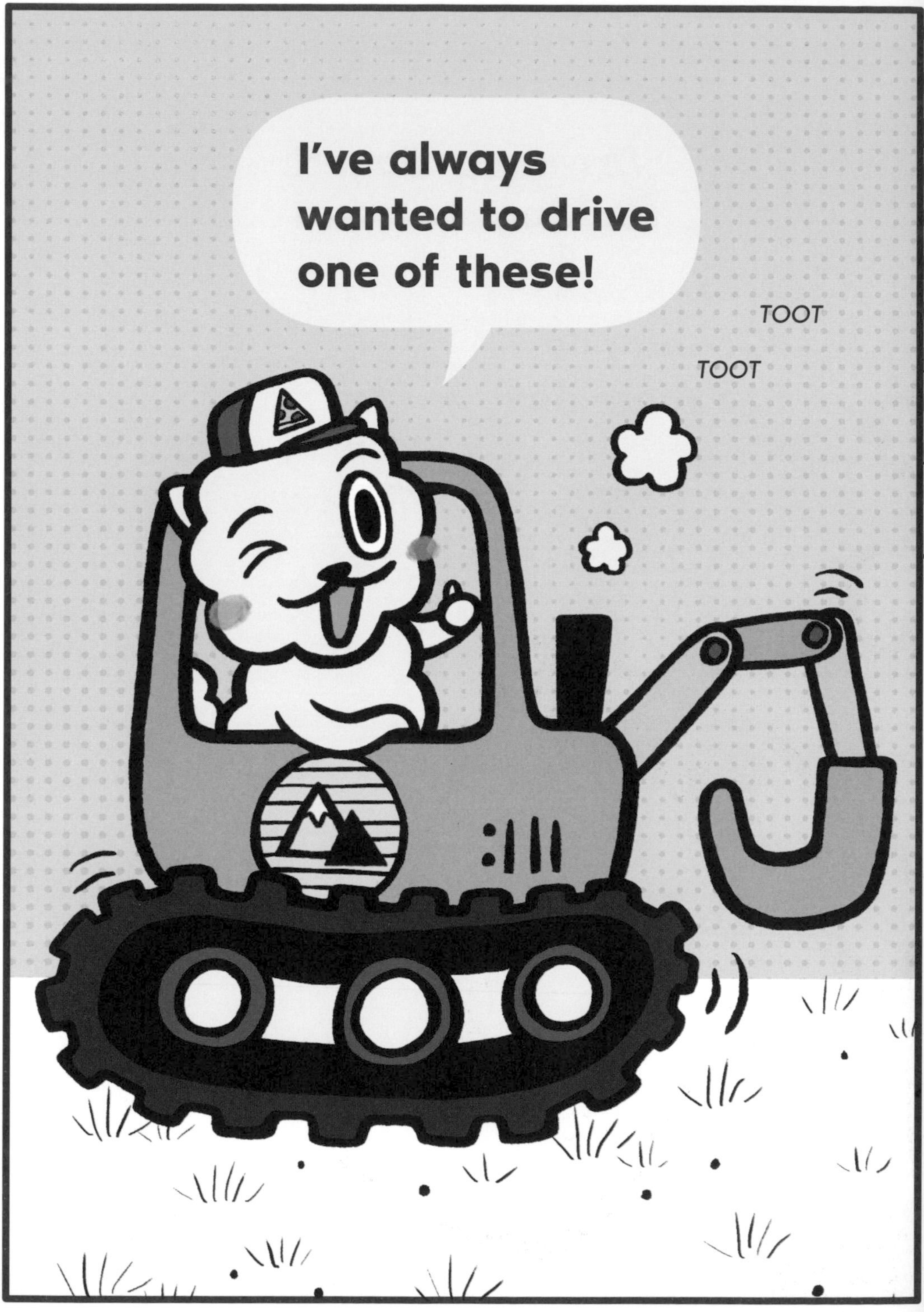
I've always wanted to drive one of these!
TOOT
TOOT

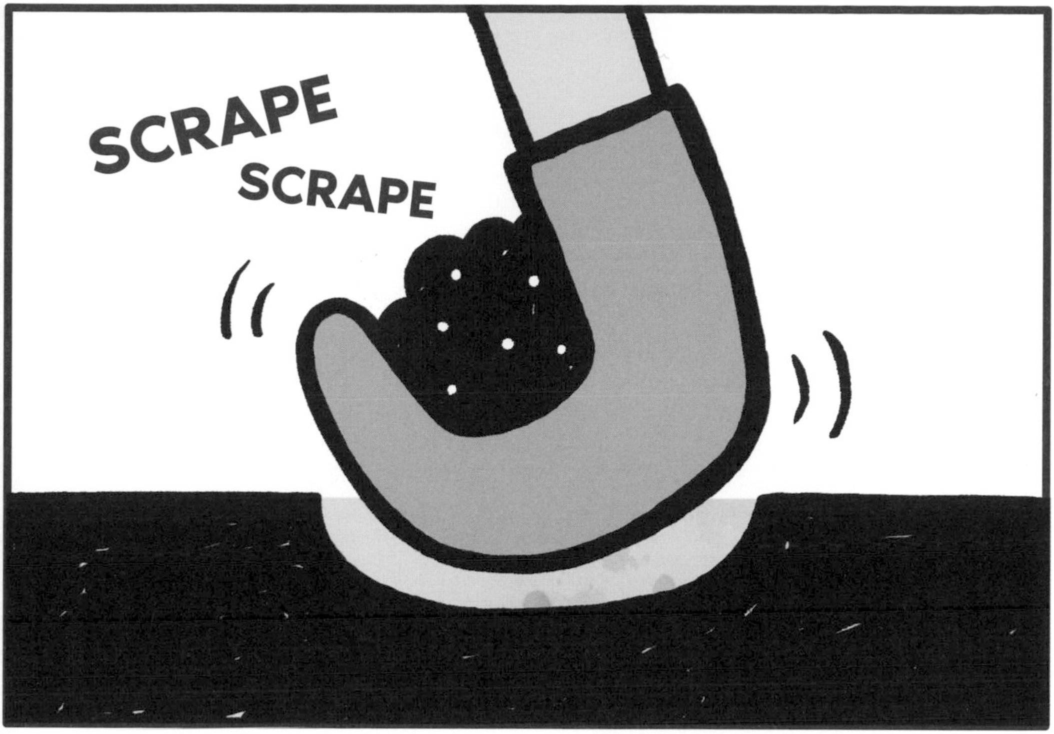
SCRAPE
SCRAPE

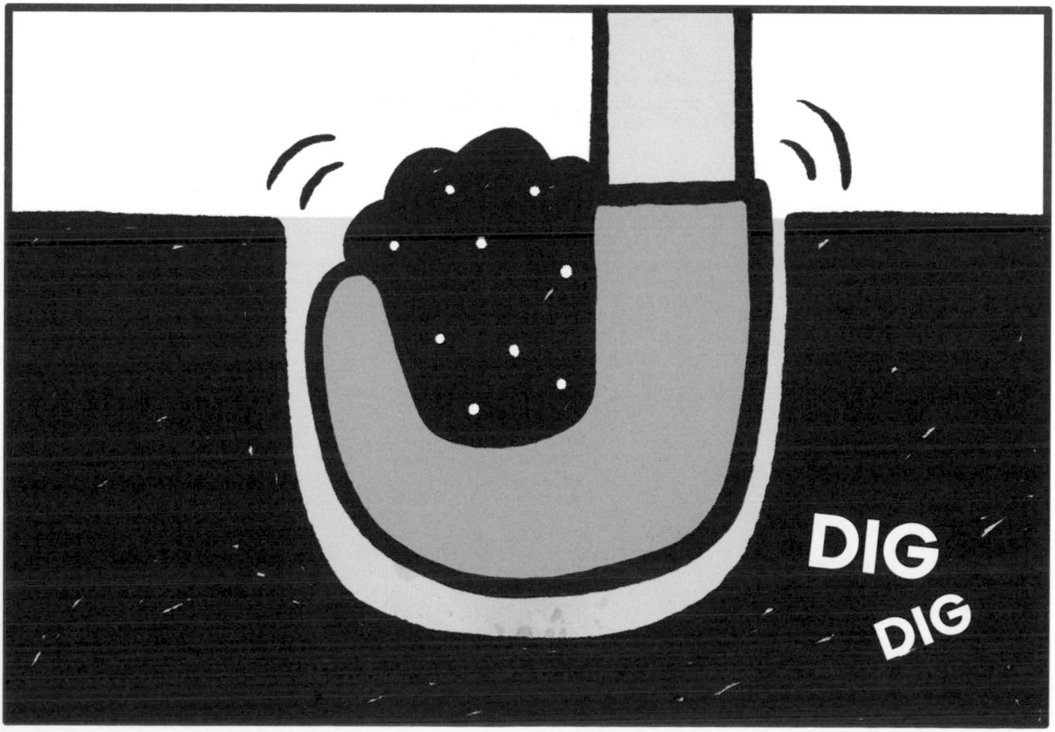
DIG
DIG

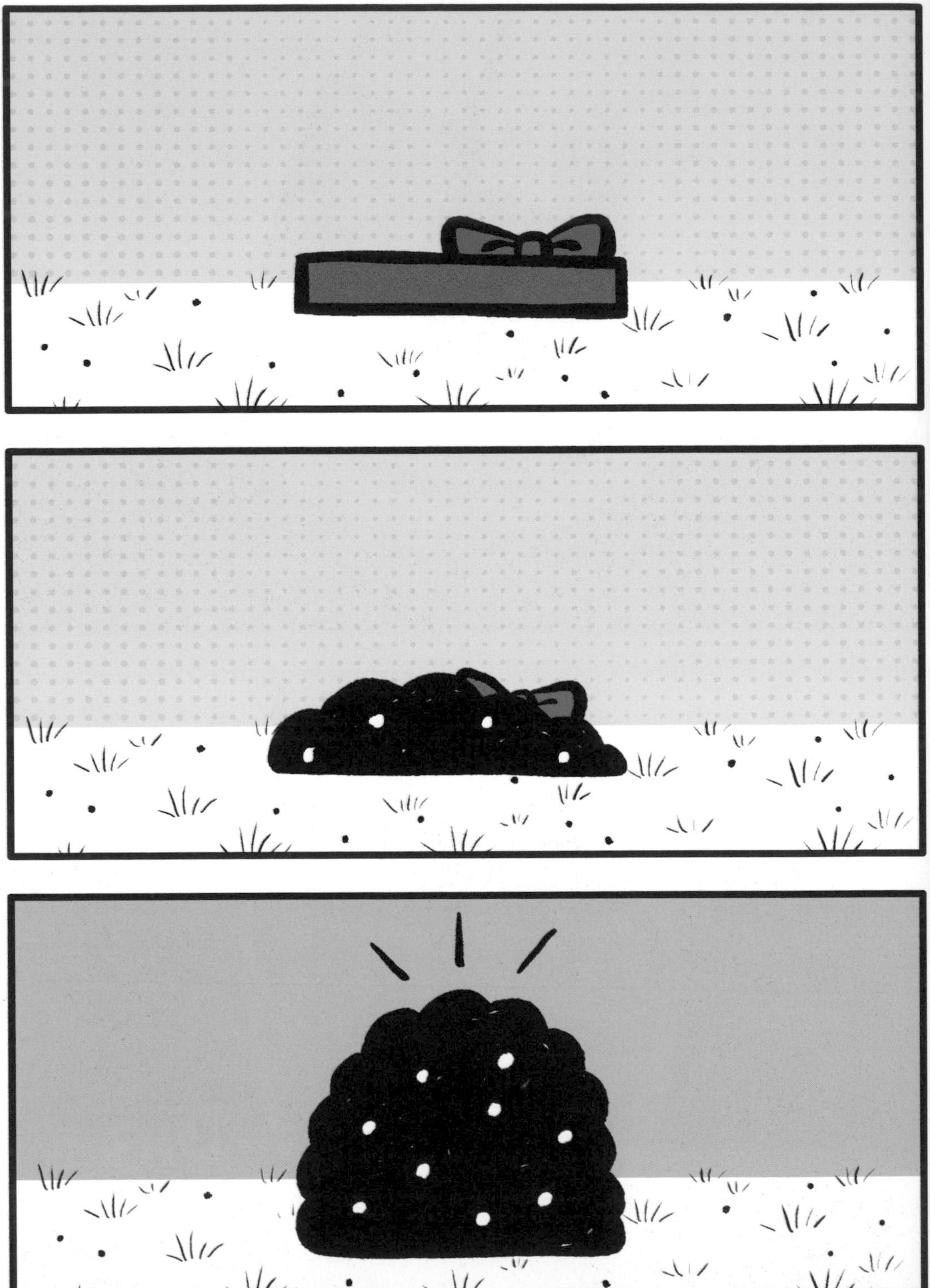

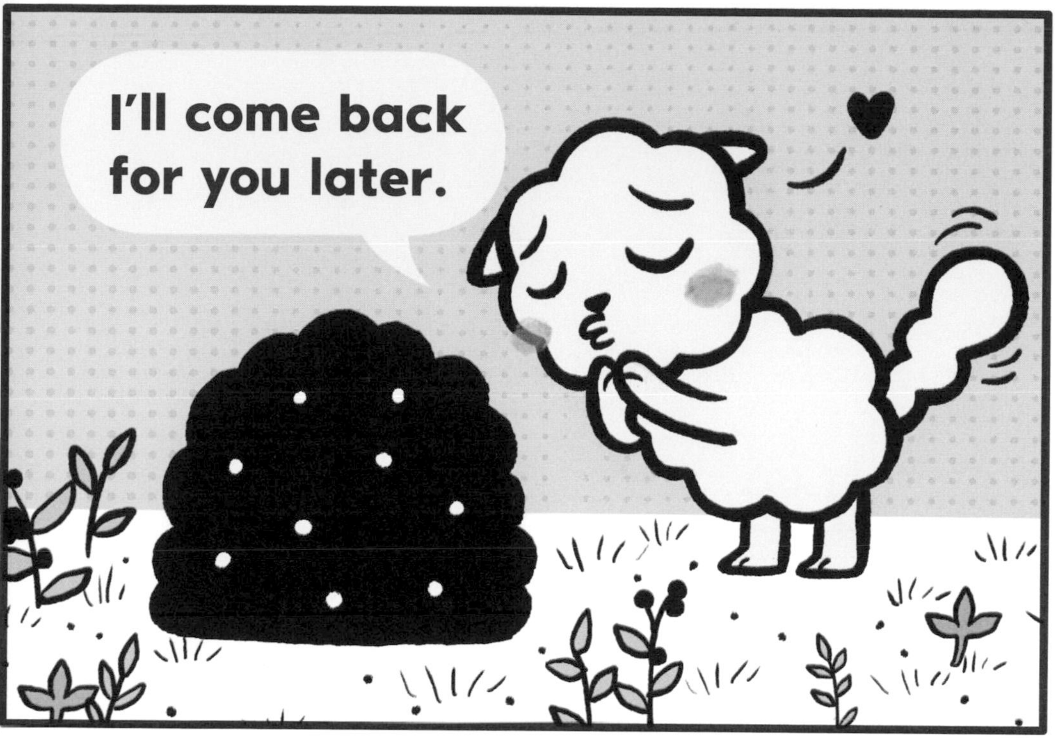
I'll come back for you later.

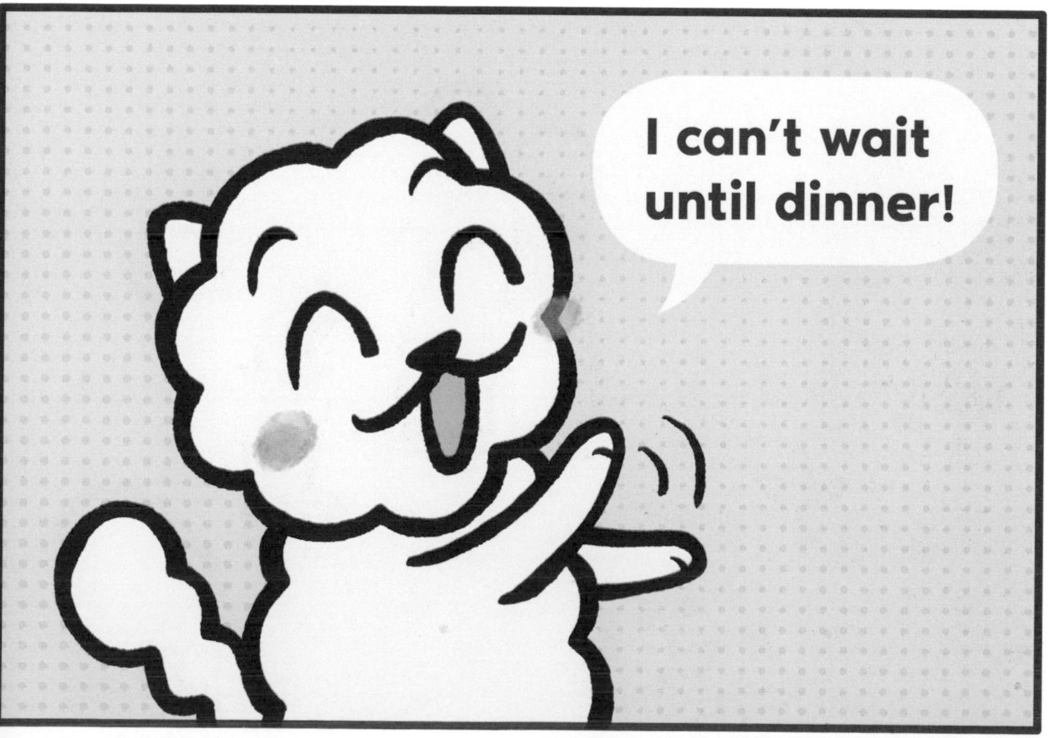
I can't wait until dinner!

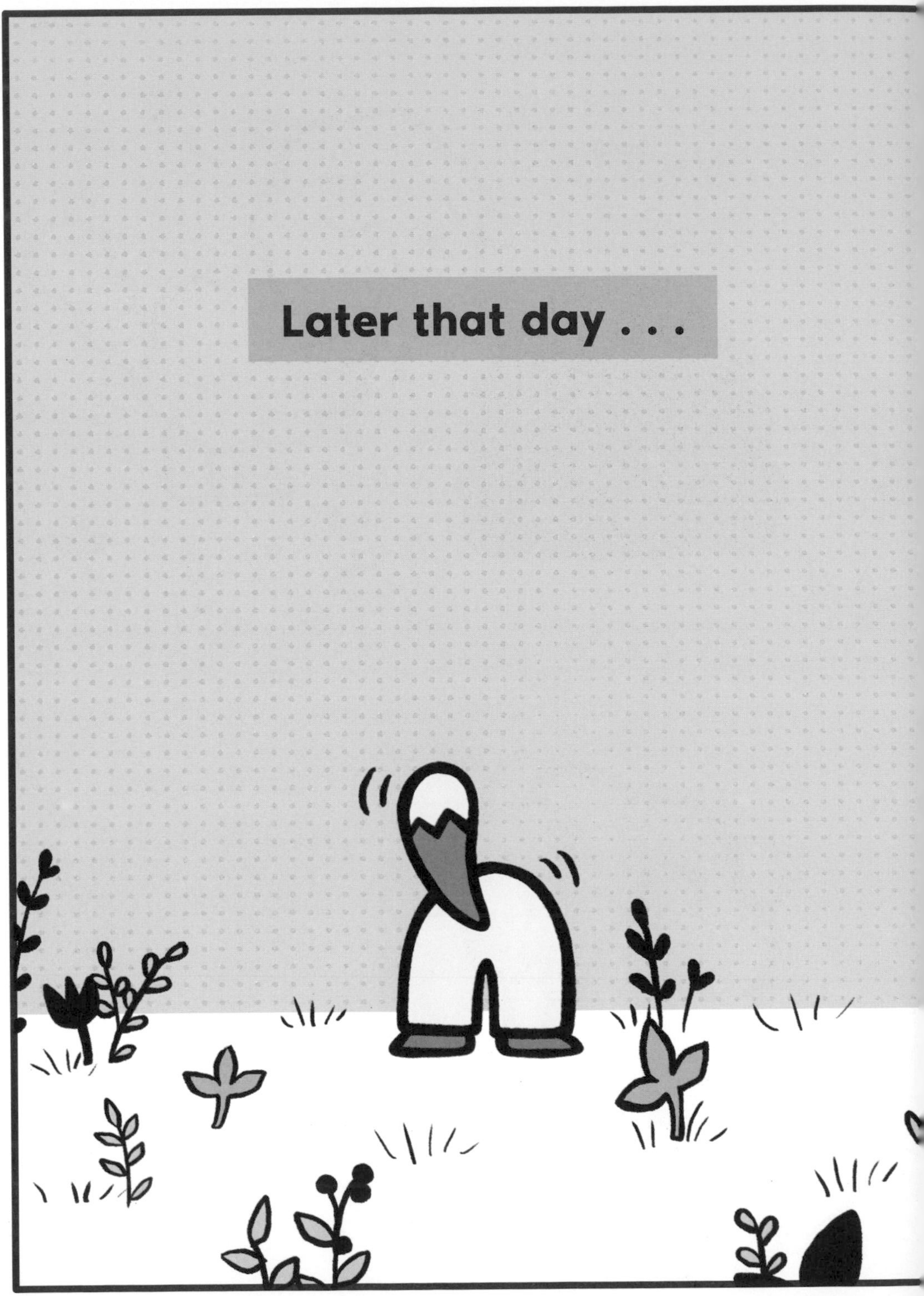
Later that day . . .

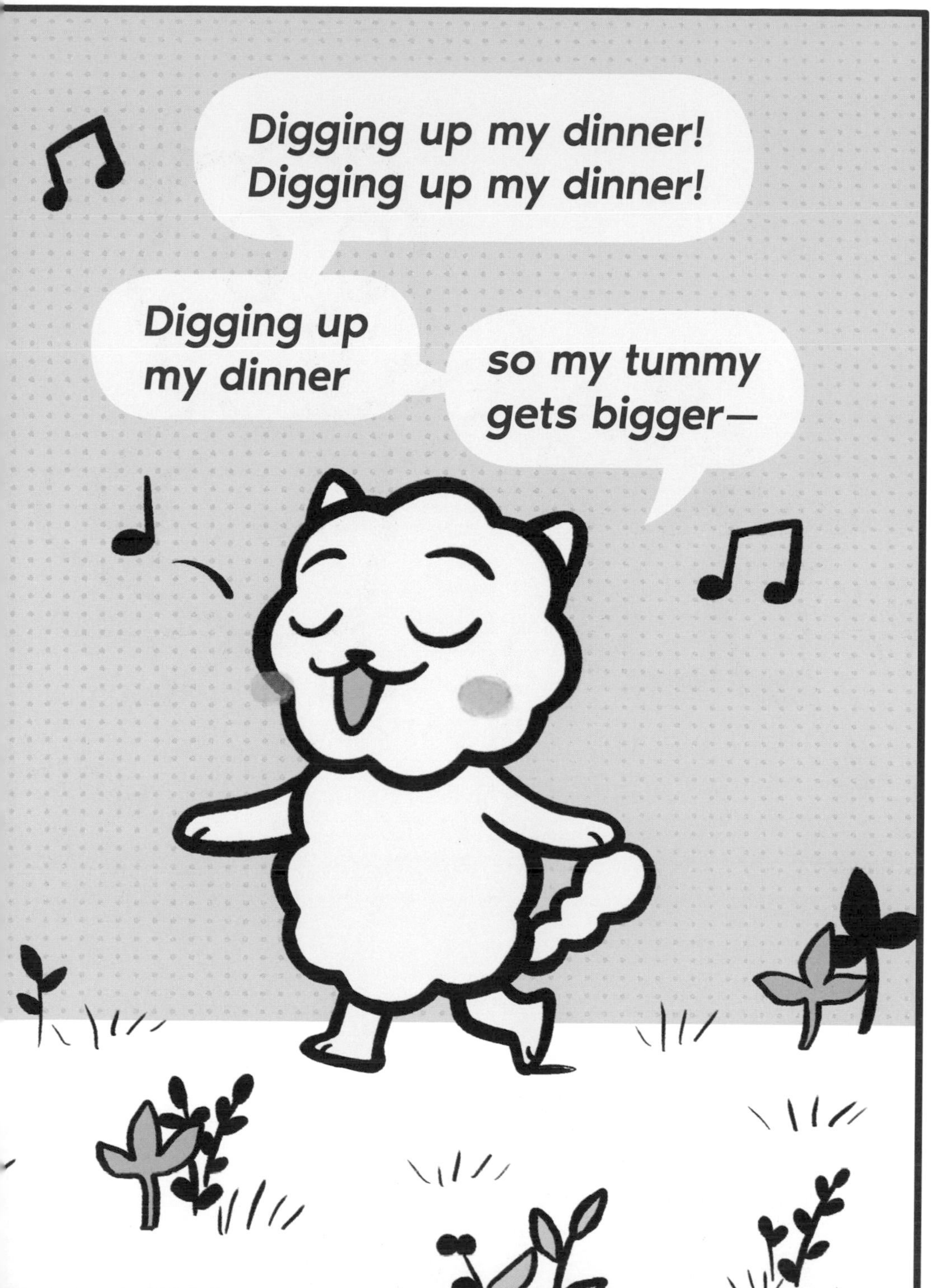
Digging up my dinner! Digging up my dinner!
Digging up my dinner
so my tummy gets bigger—

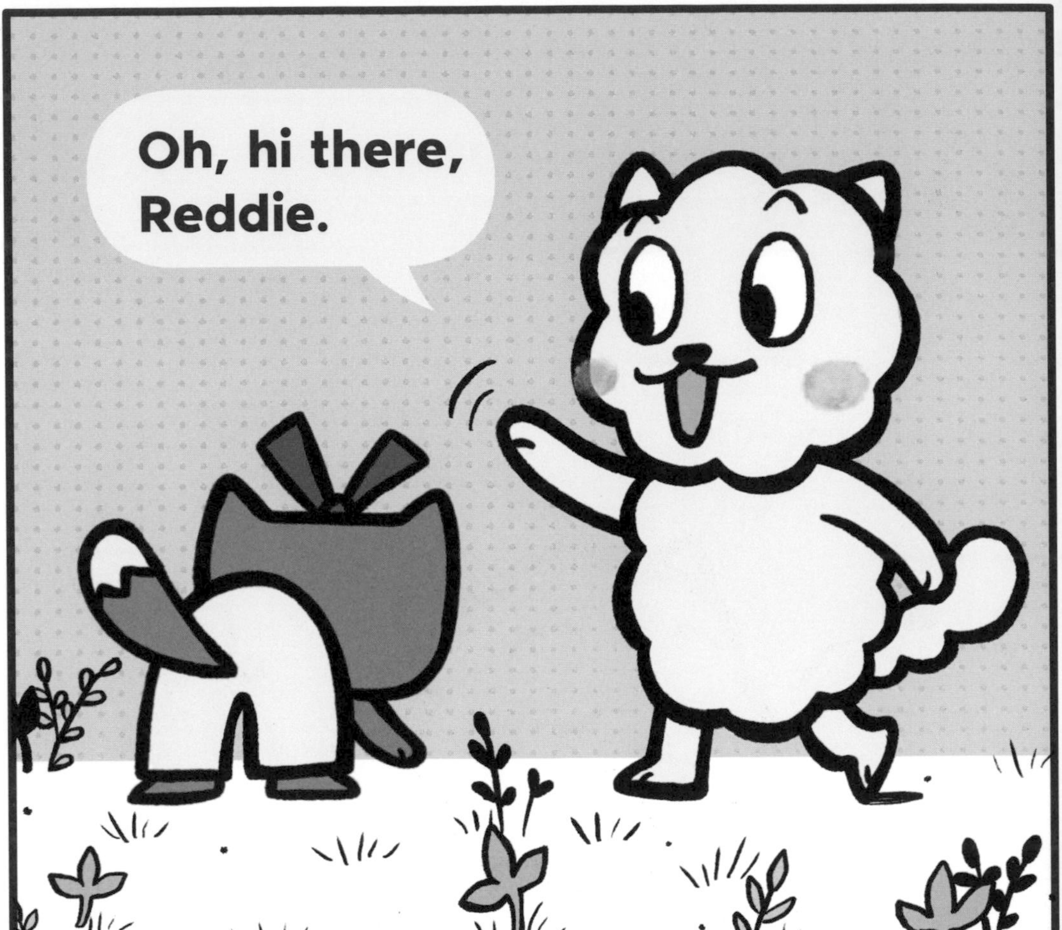
Oh, hi there, Reddie.

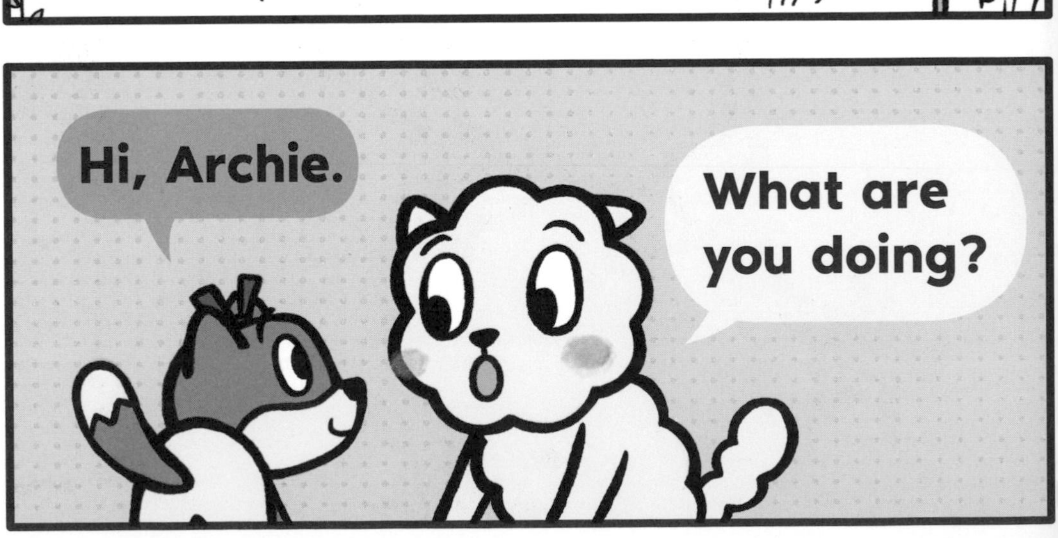
Hi, Archie.
What are you doing?

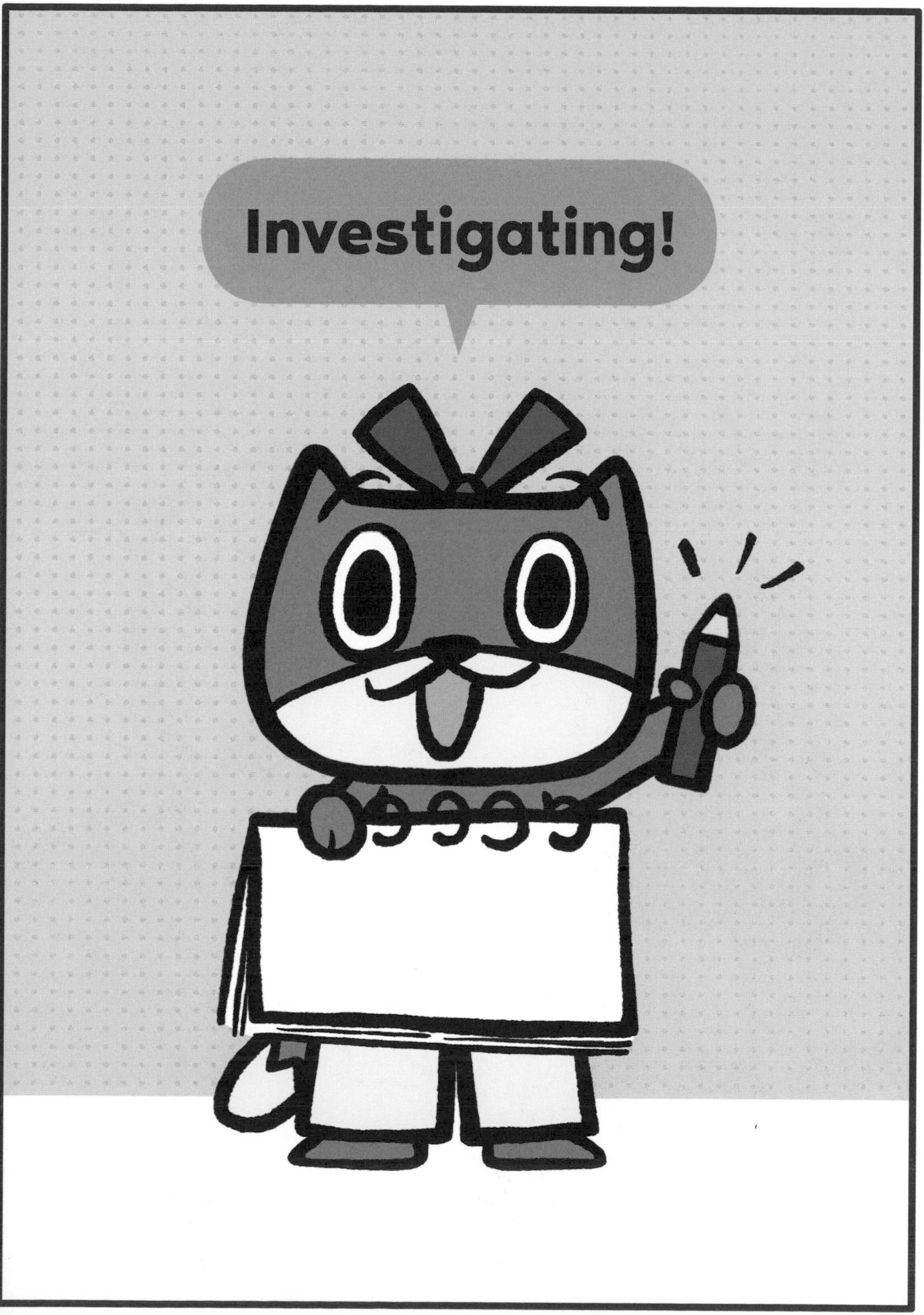
Investigating!

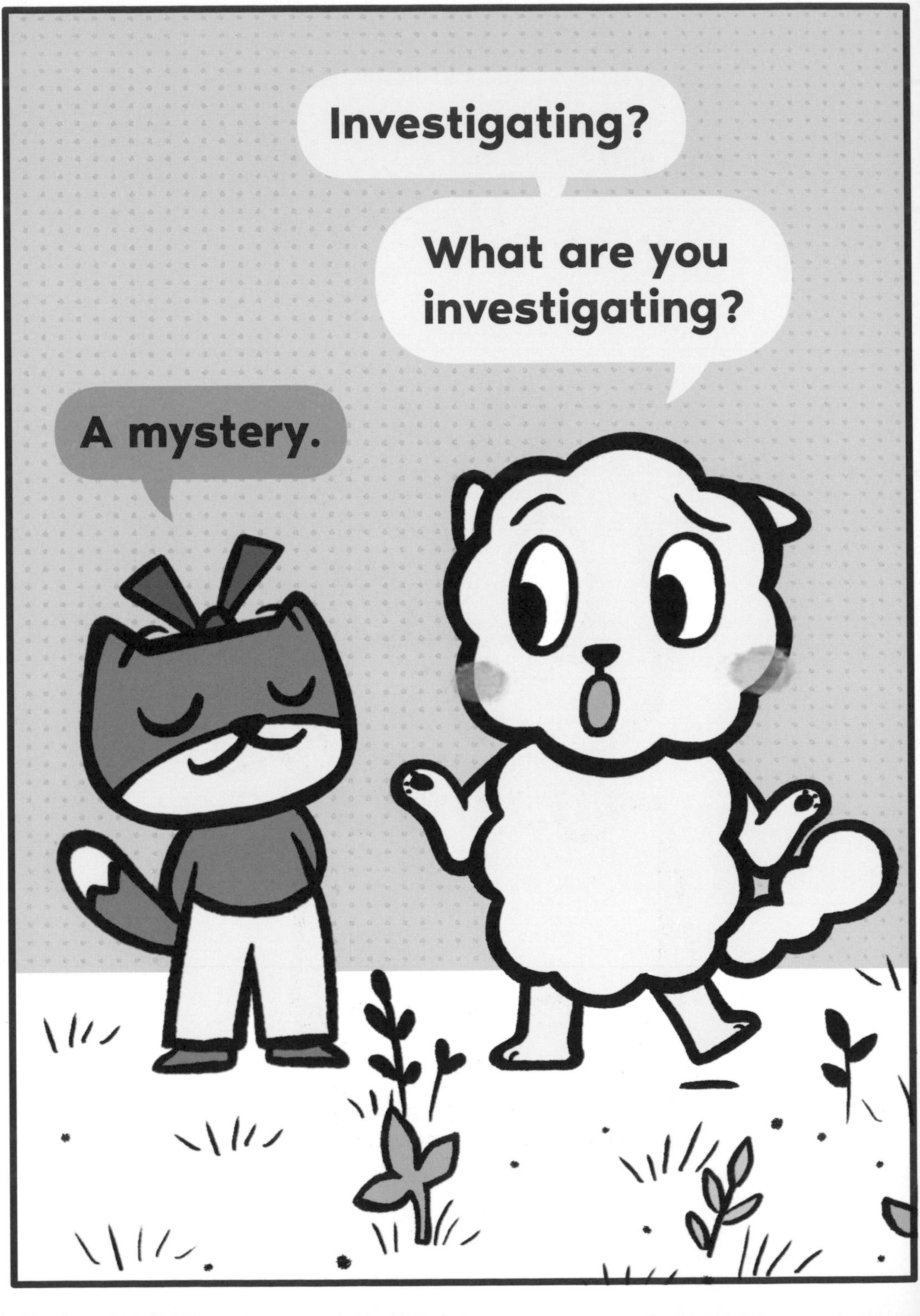
Investigating?
What are you investigating?
A mystery.

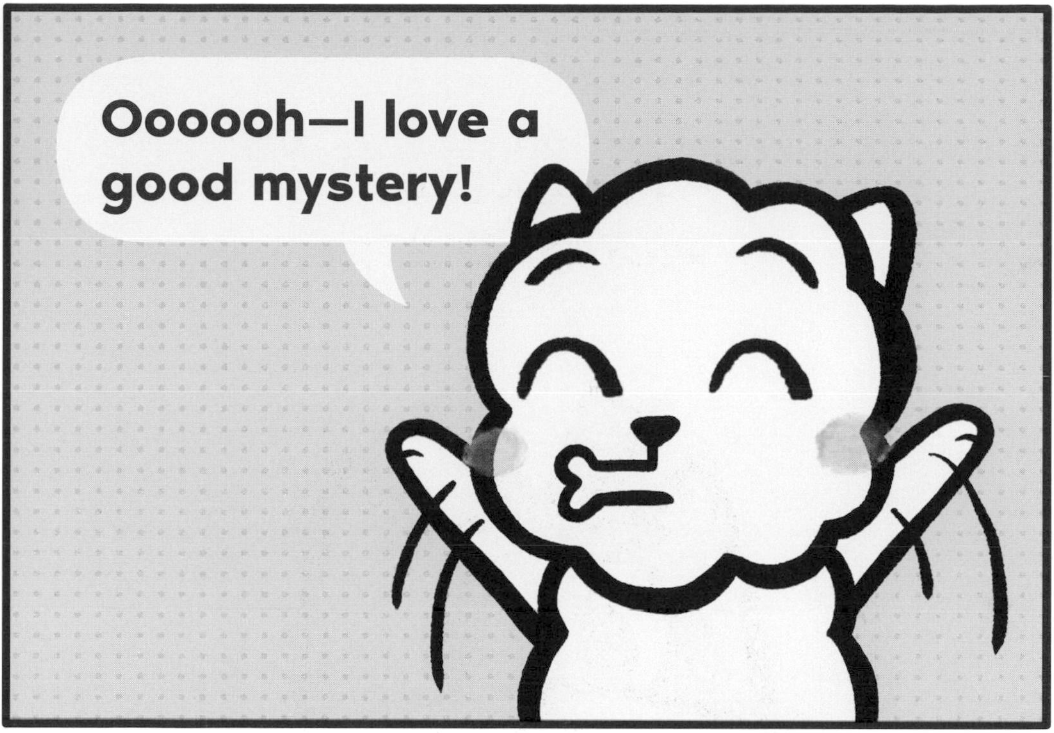
Oooooh—I love a good mystery!

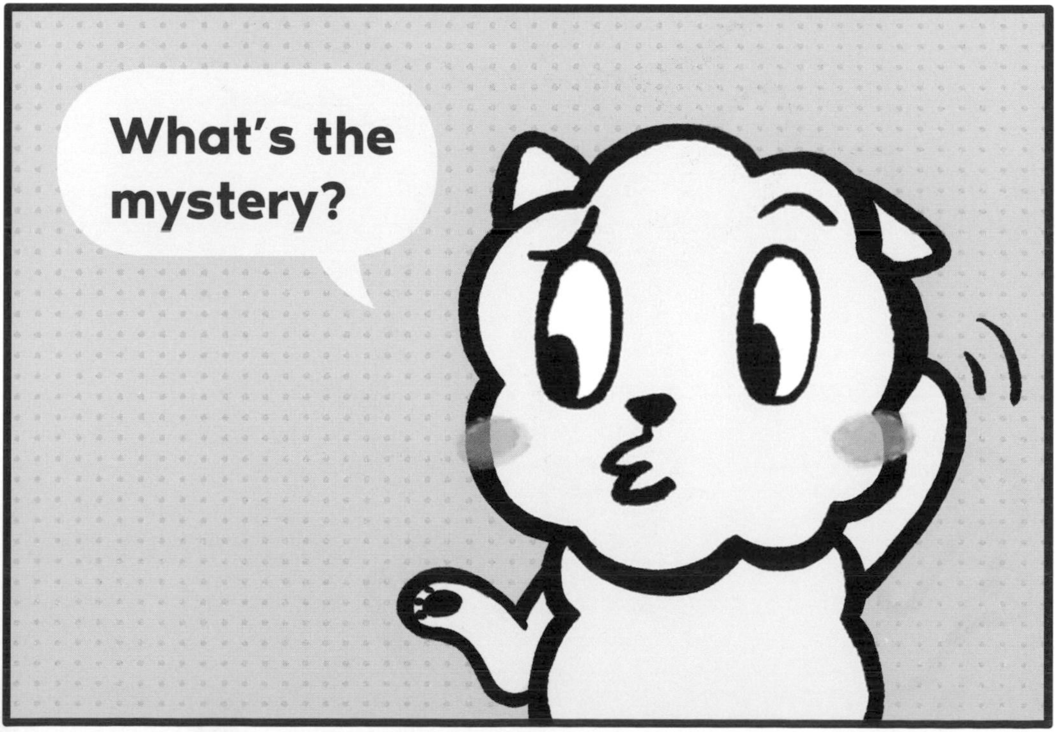
What's the mystery?

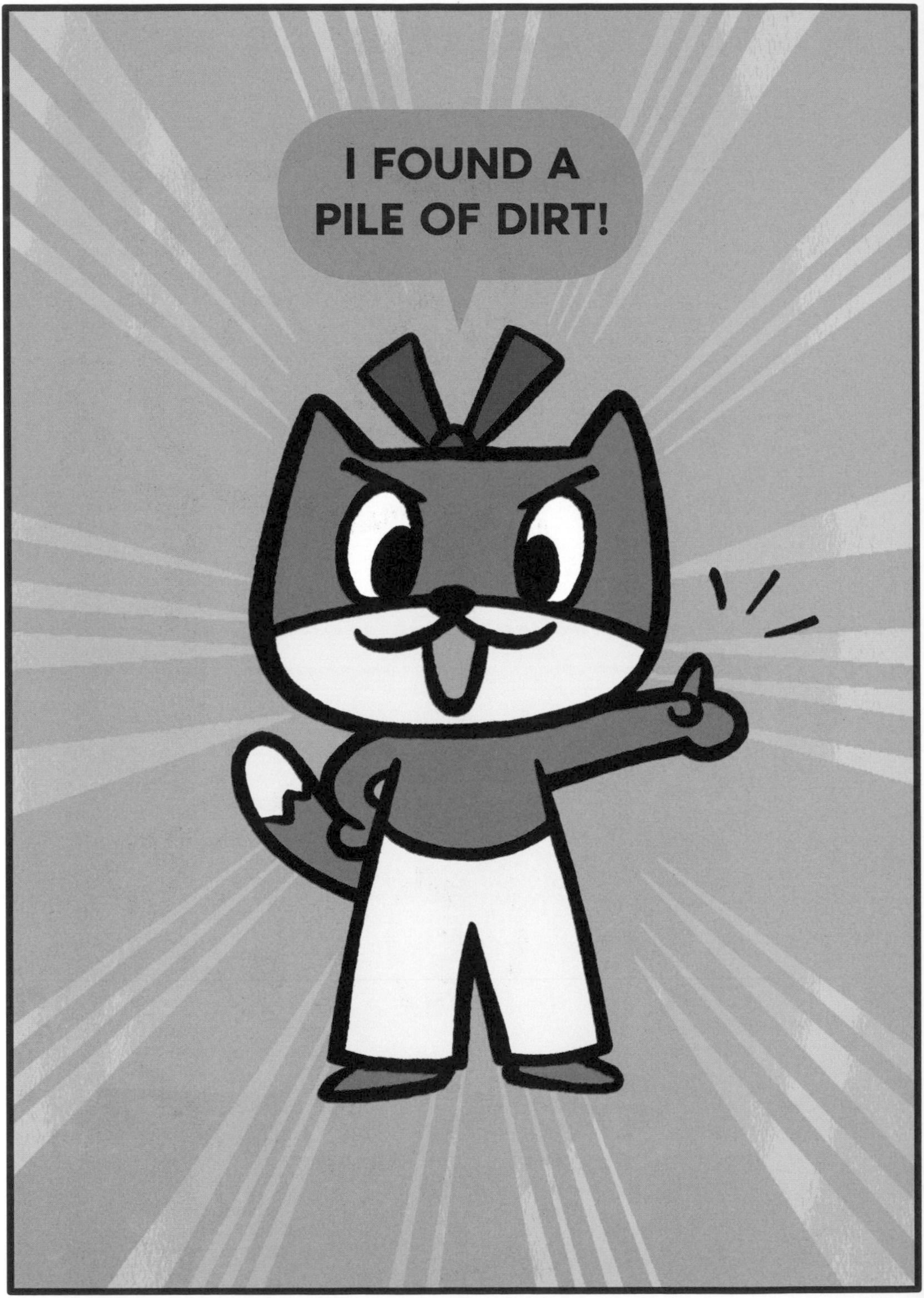
I FOUND A PILE OF DIRT!

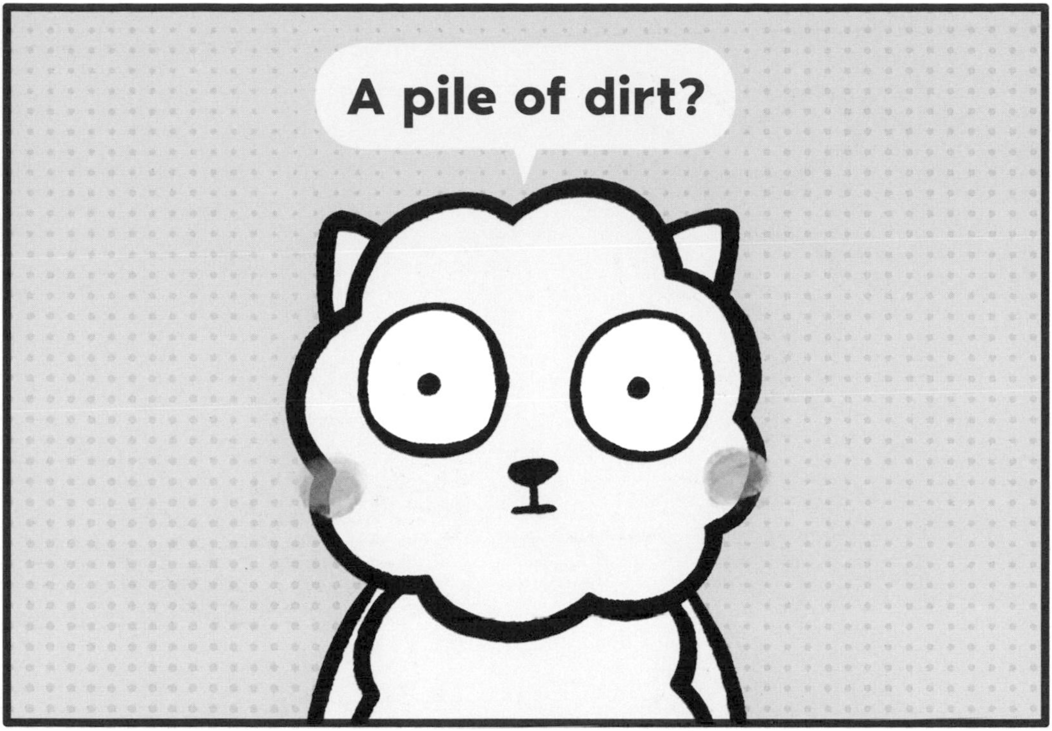
A pile of dirt?

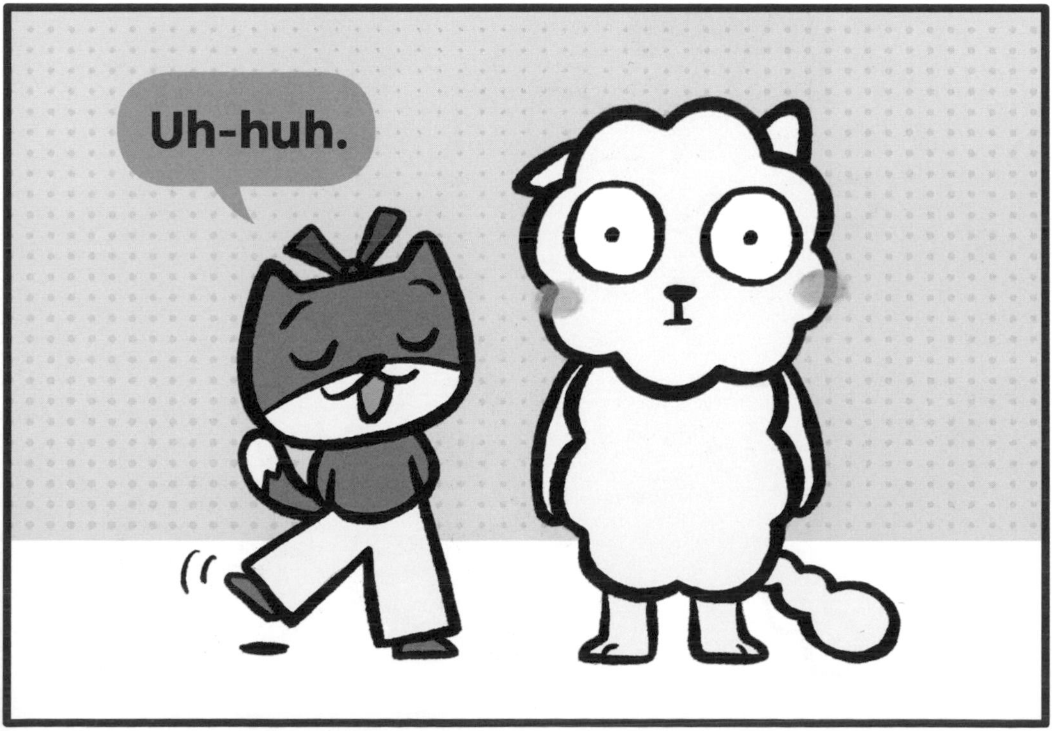
Uh-huh.

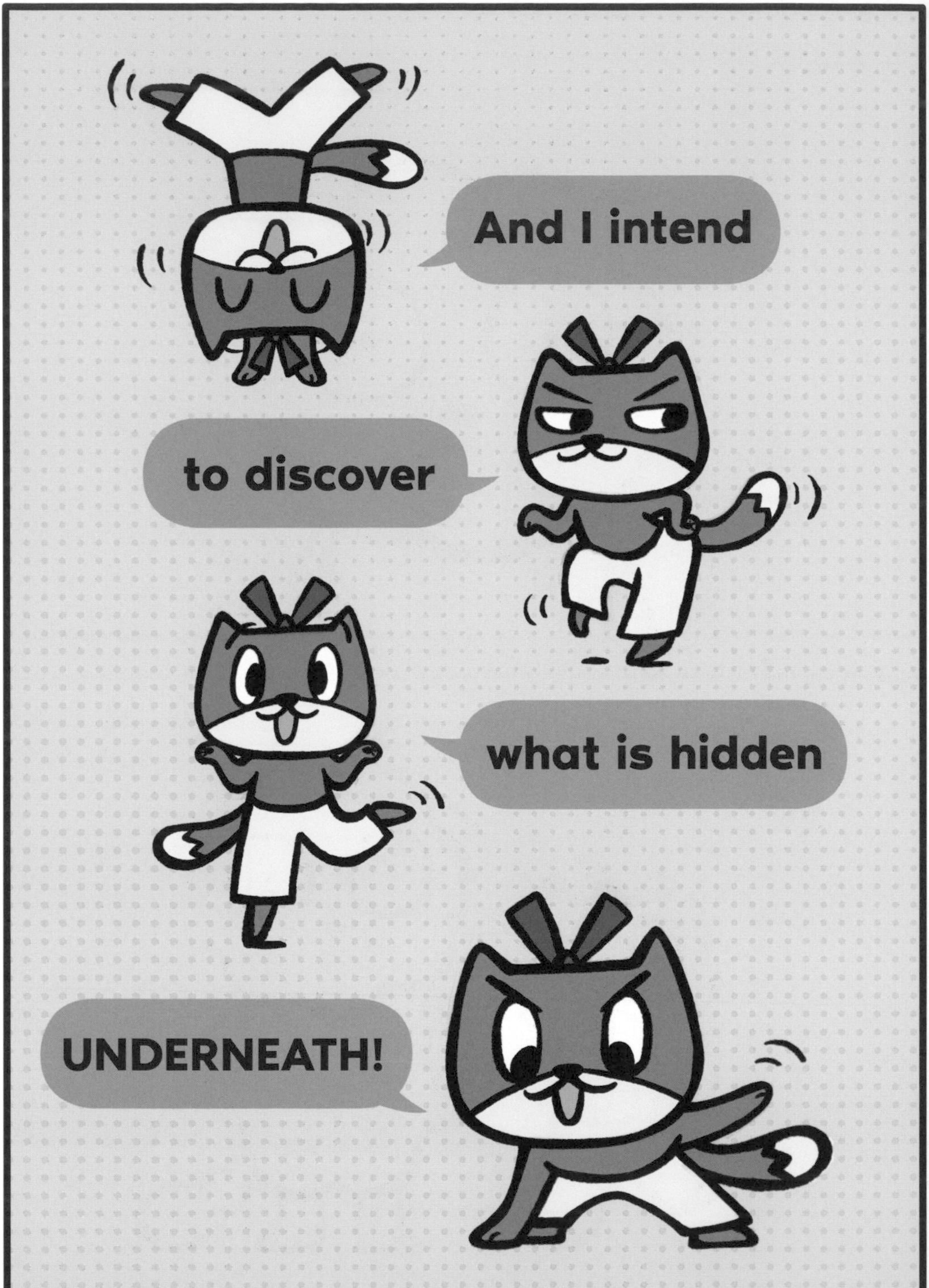
And I intend
to discover
what is hidden
UNDERNEATH!

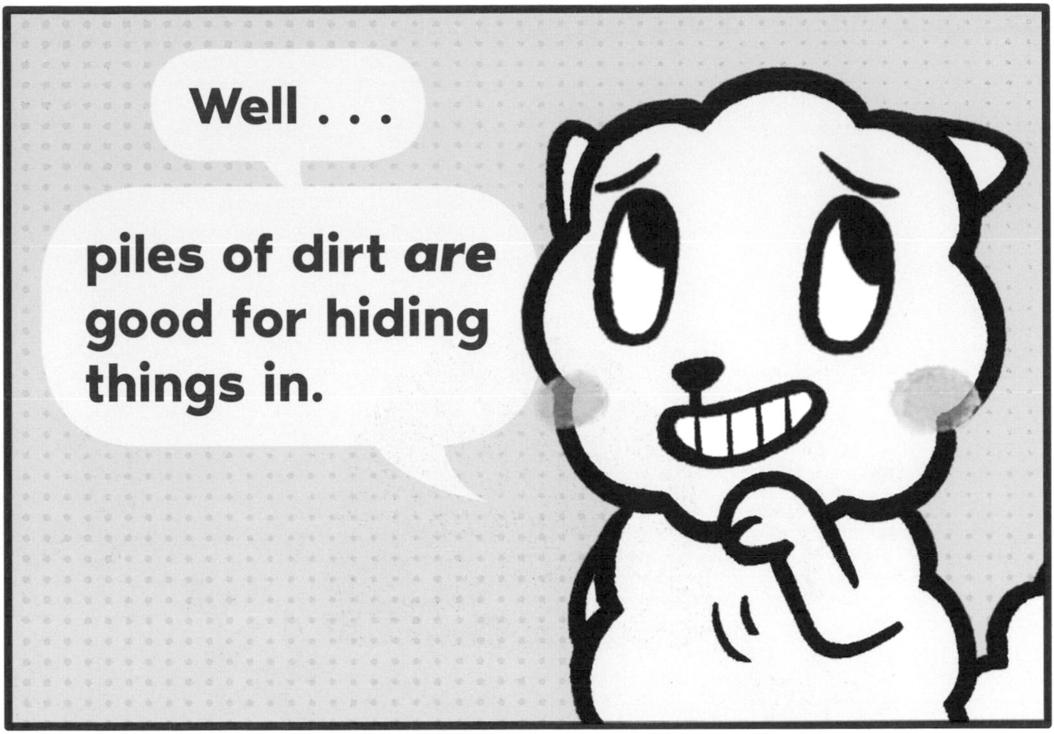
Well . . .
piles of dirt *are* good for hiding things in.

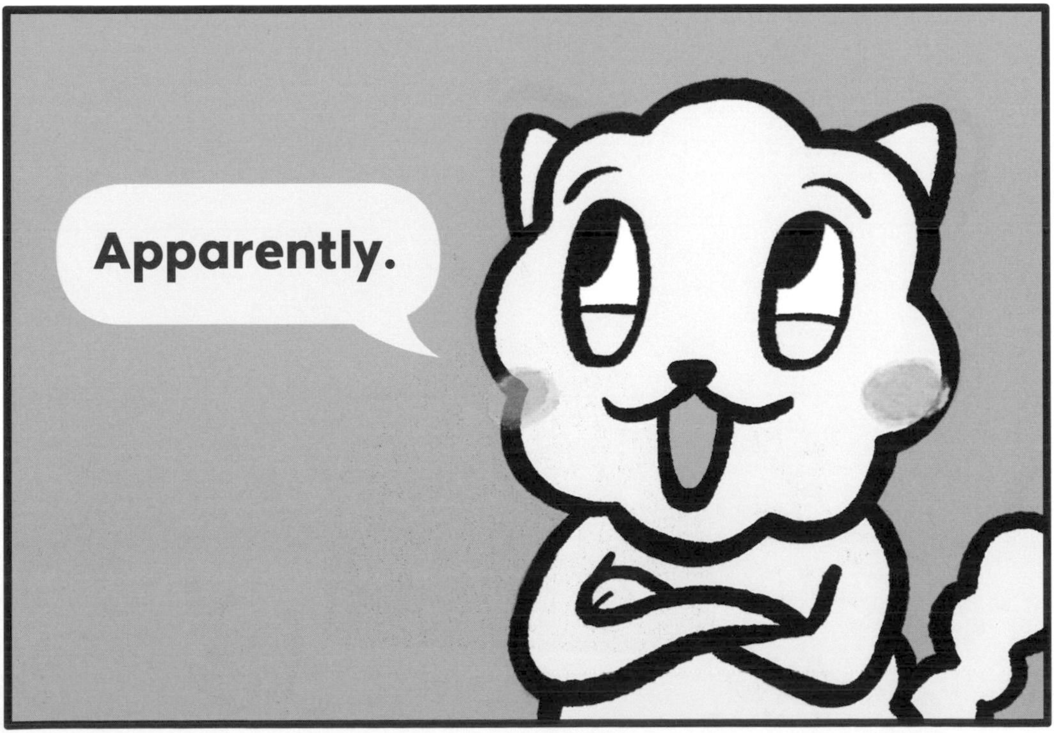
Apparently.

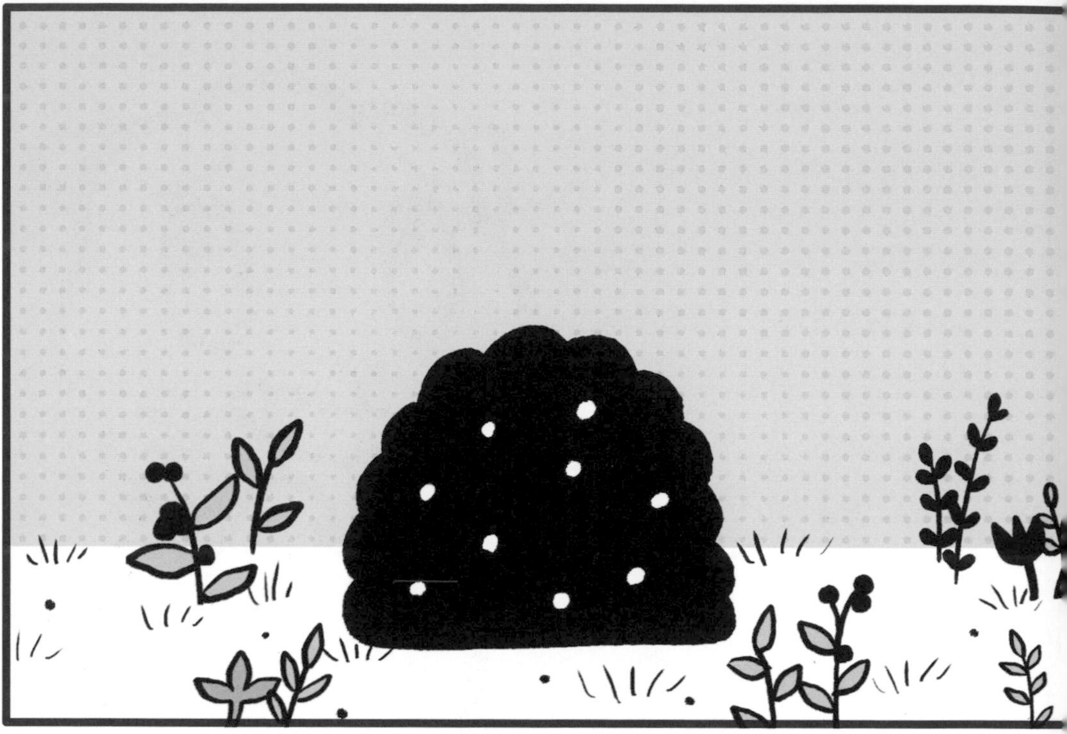

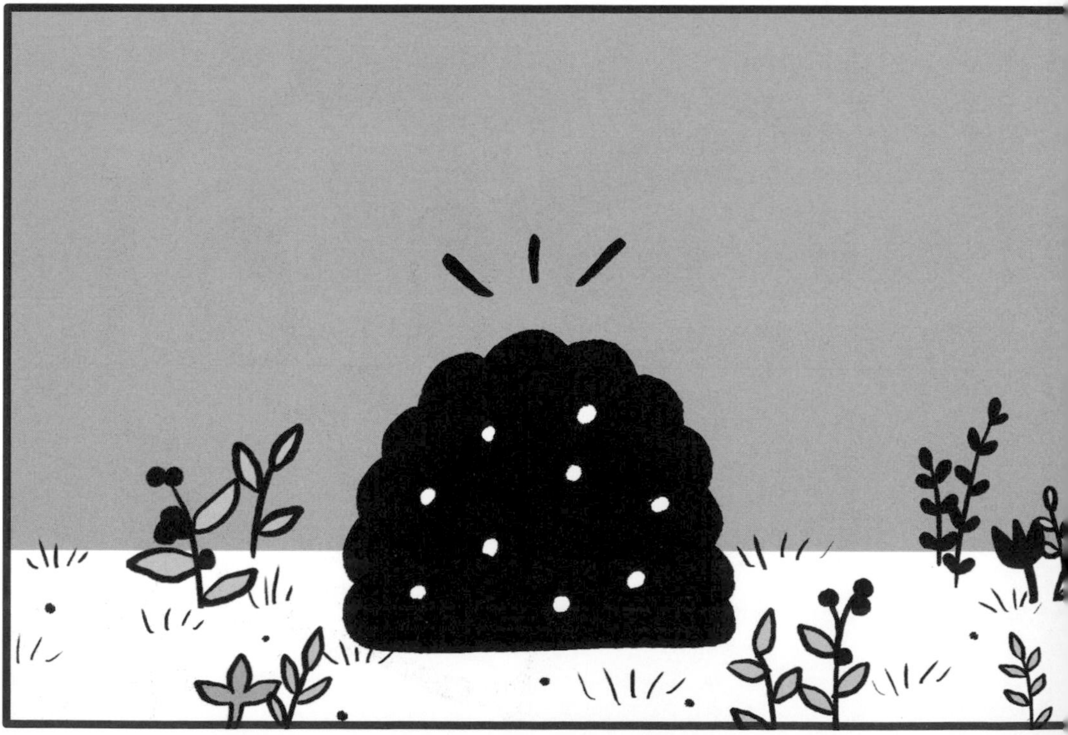

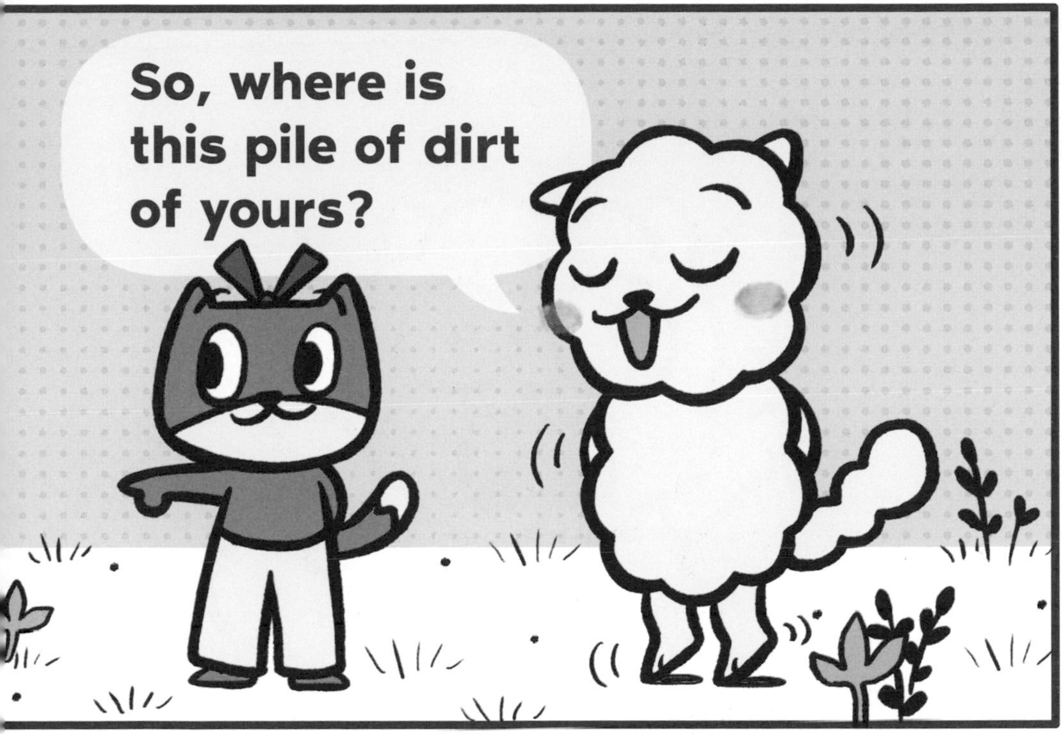
So, where is this pile of dirt of yours?

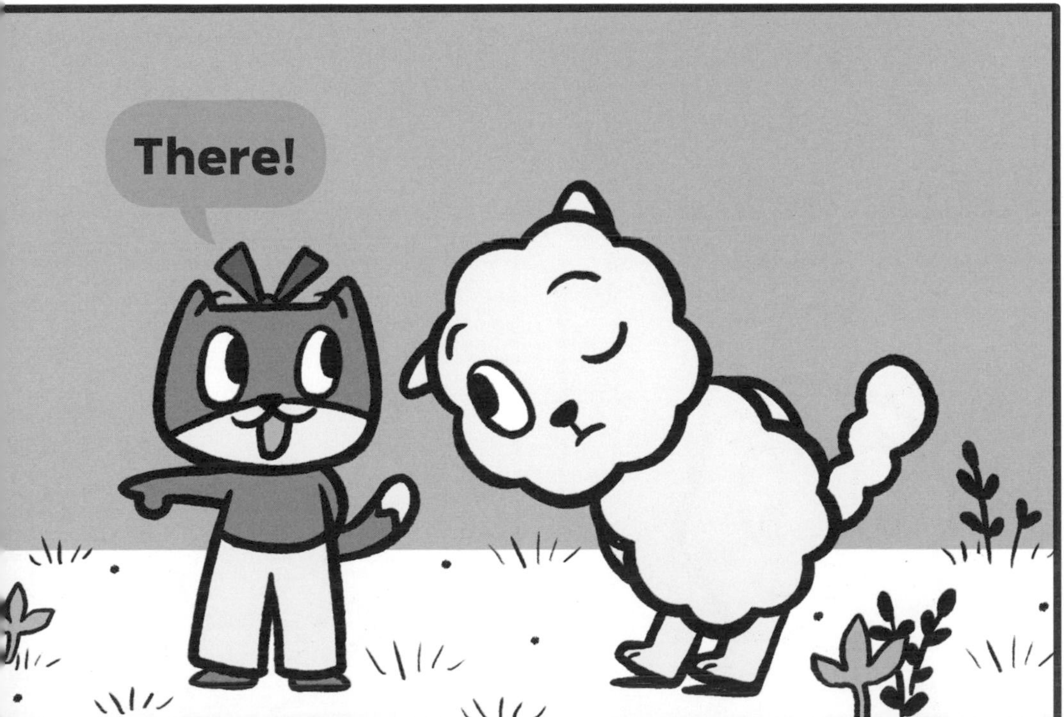
There!

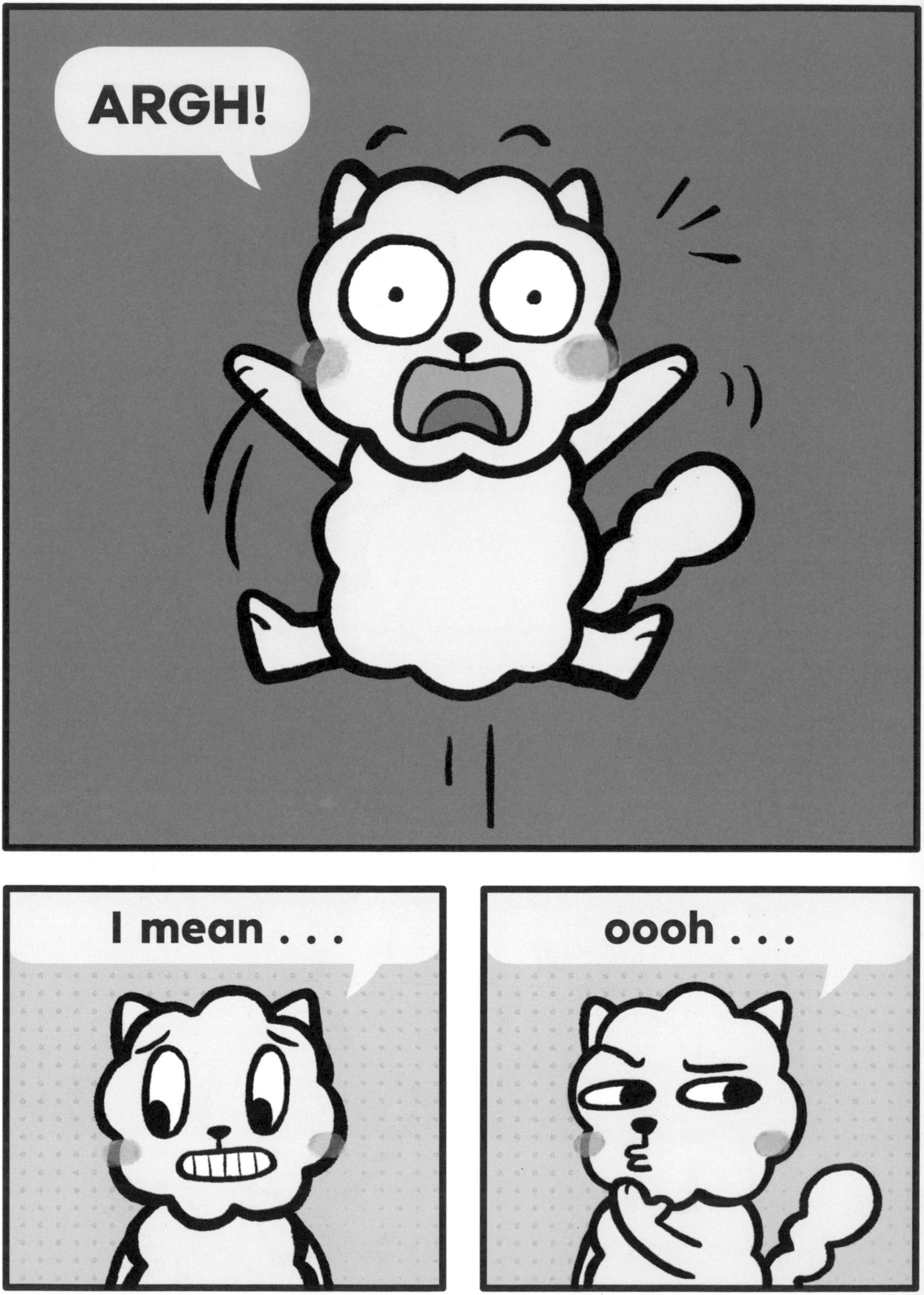
ARGH!
I mean . . .
oooh . . .

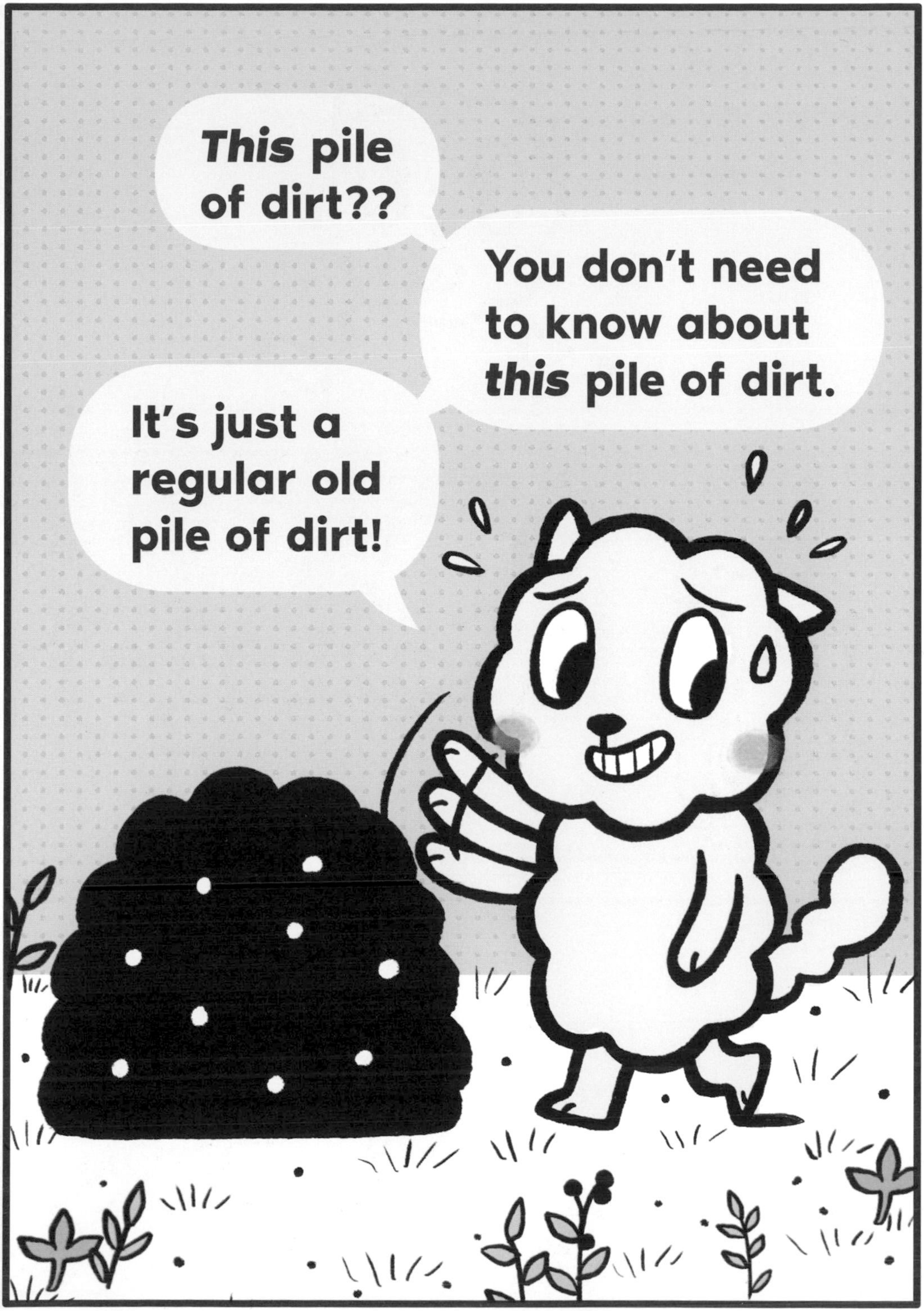
This pile of dirt??
You don't need to know about *this* pile of dirt.
It's just a regular old pile of dirt!

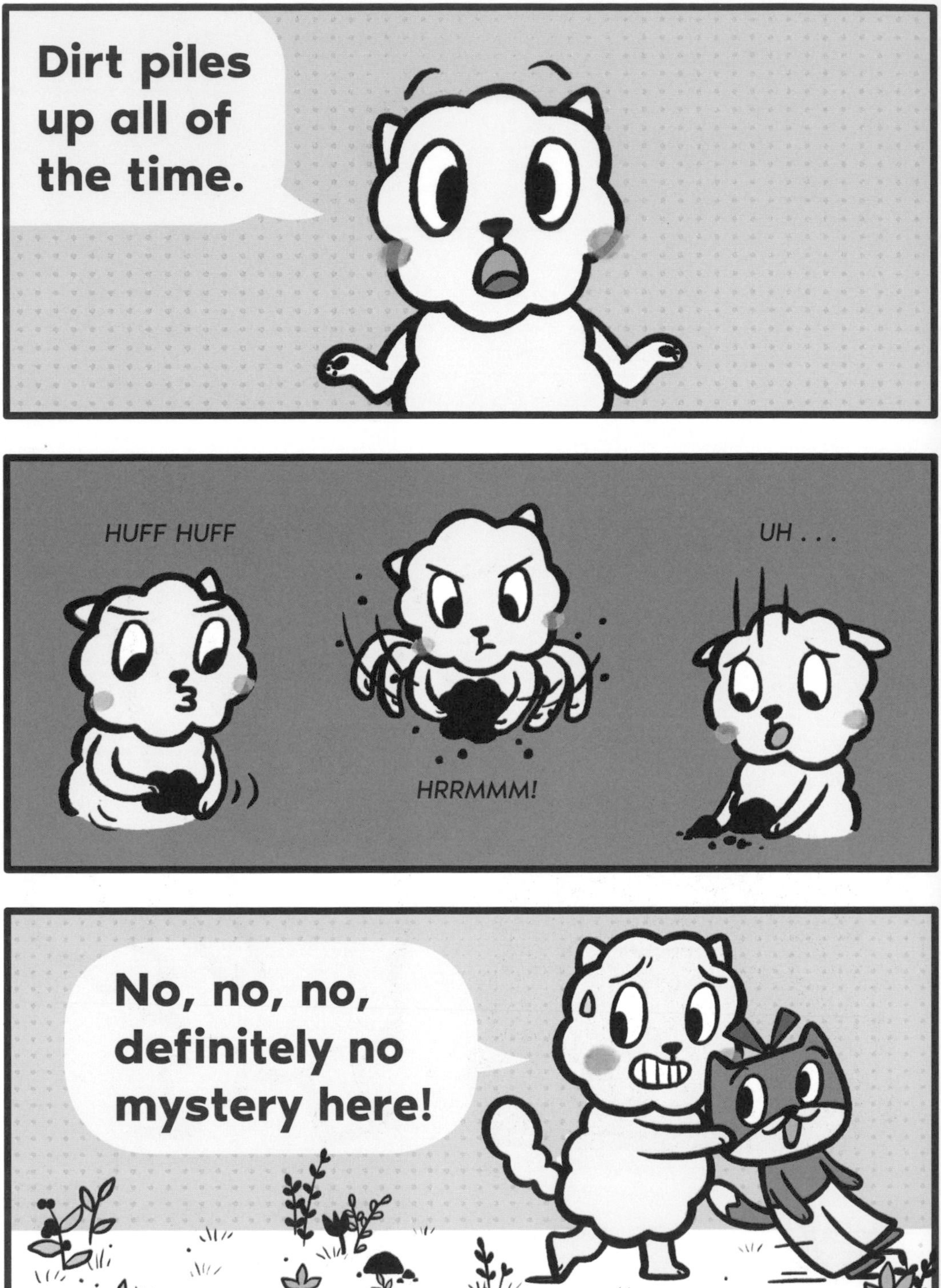
Dirt piles up all of the time.
HUFF HUFF
HRRMMM!
UH . . .
No, no, no, definitely no mystery here!

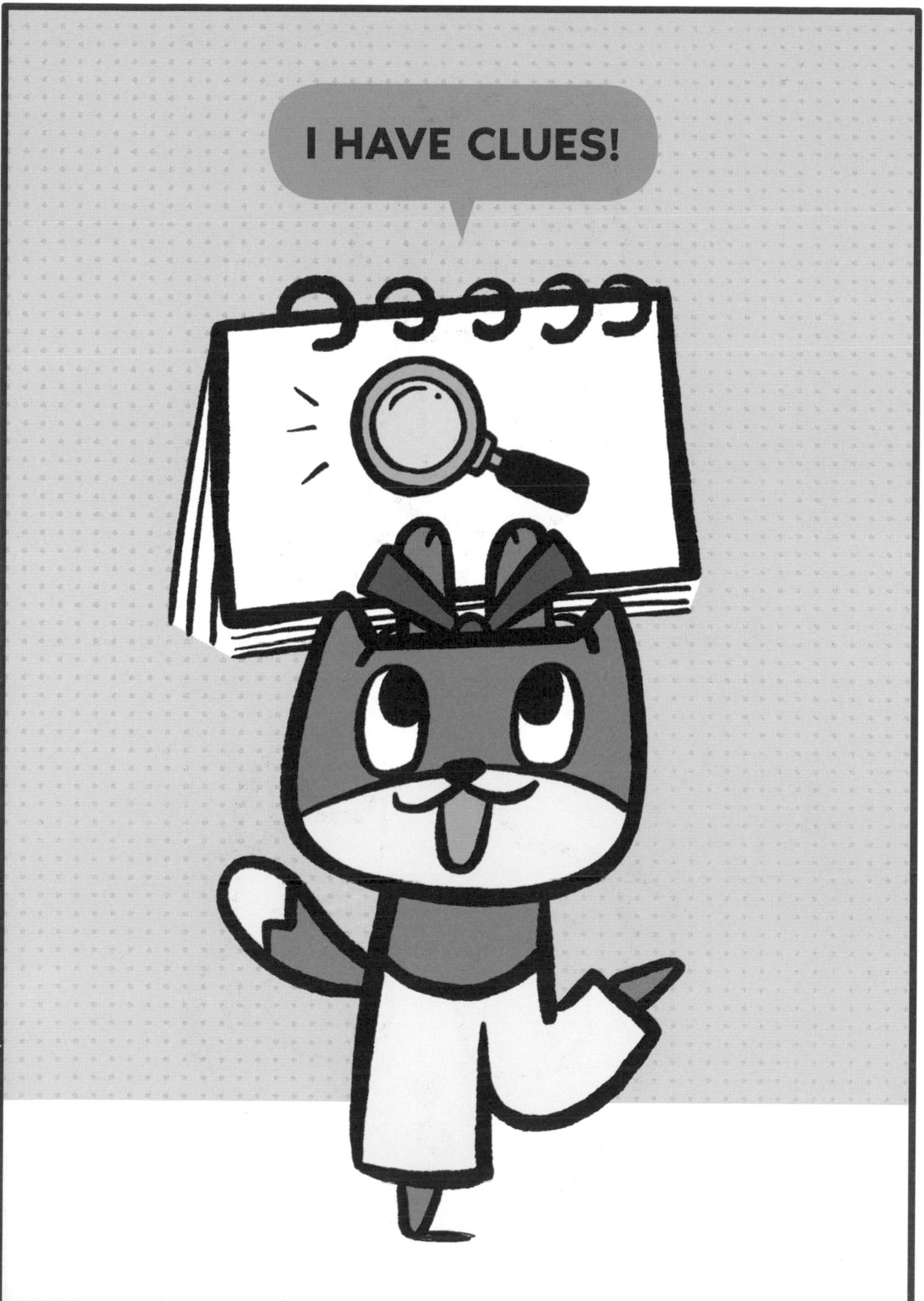
I HAVE CLUES!

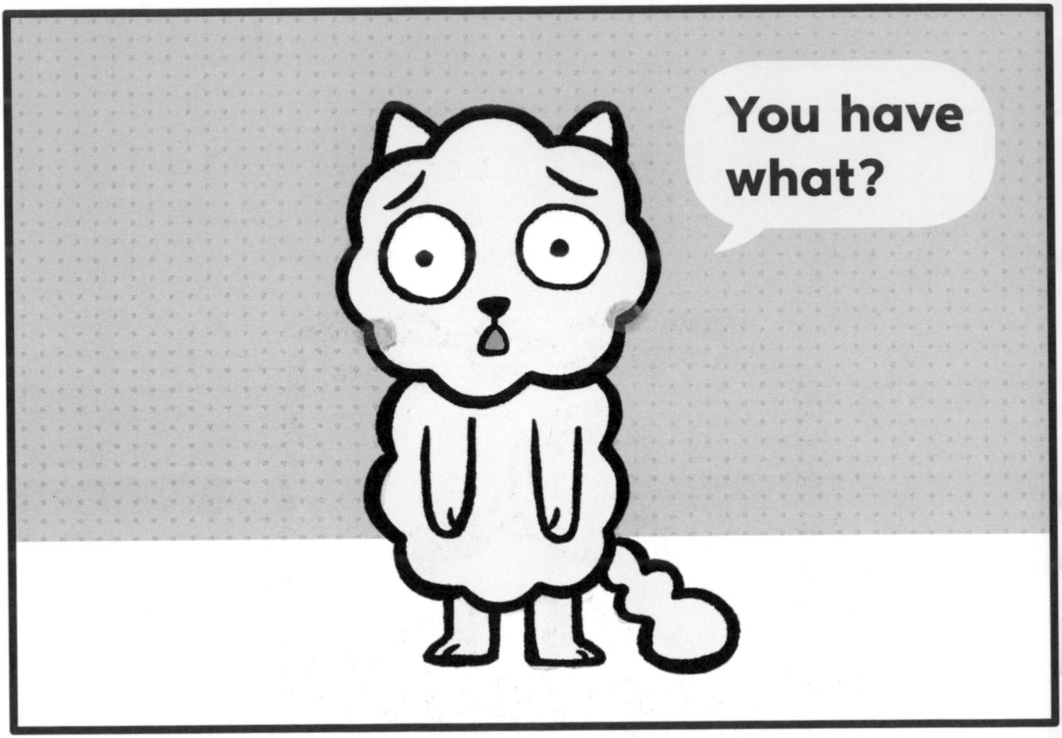
You have what?

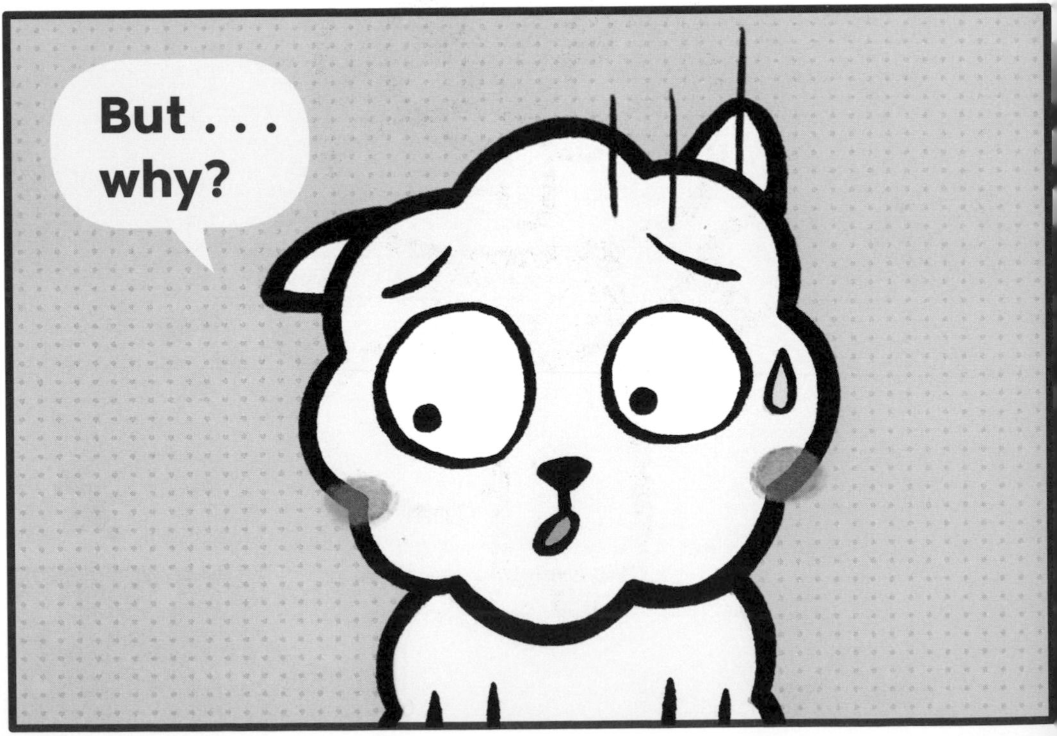
But . . . why?

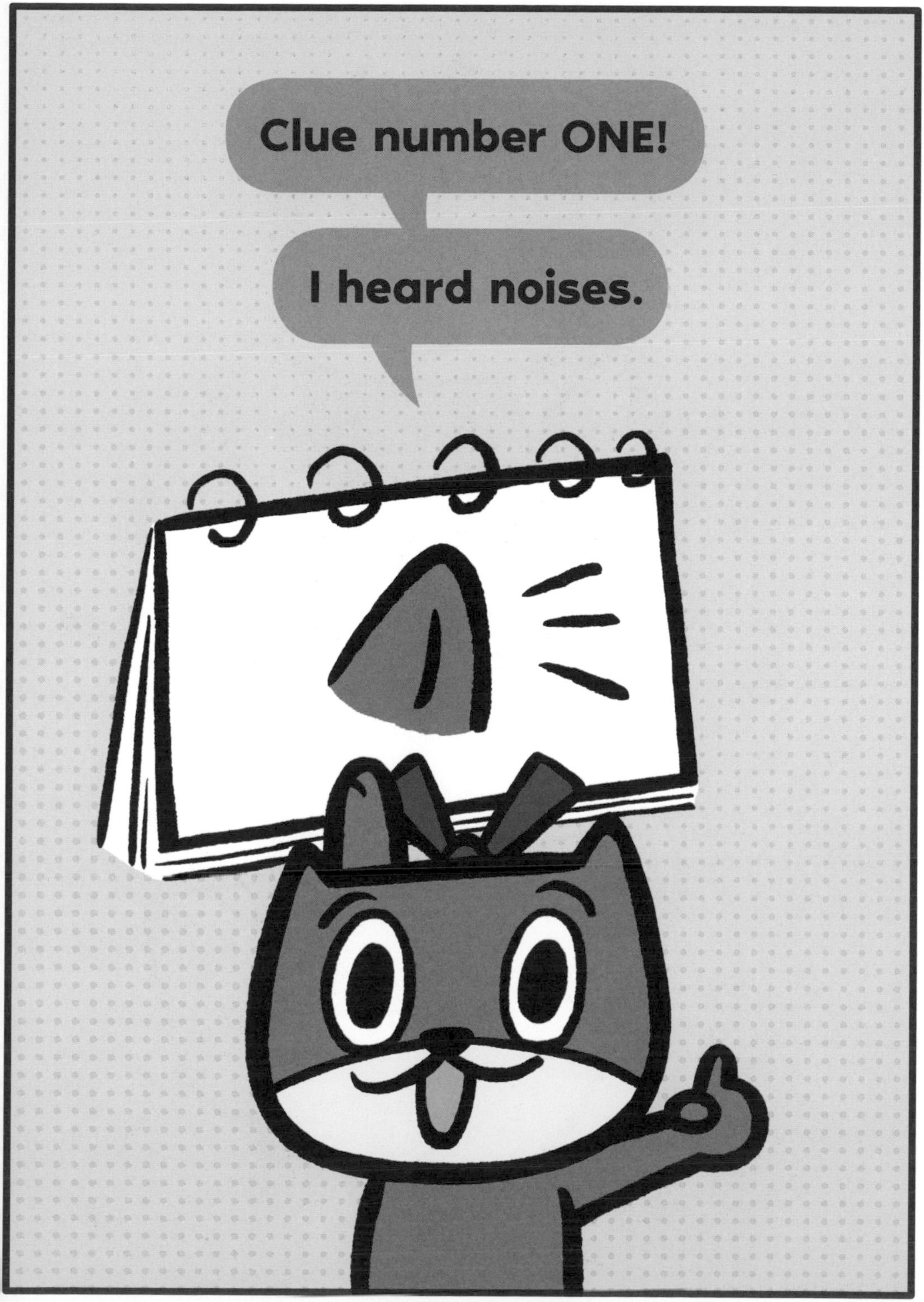
Clue number ONE!
I heard noises.

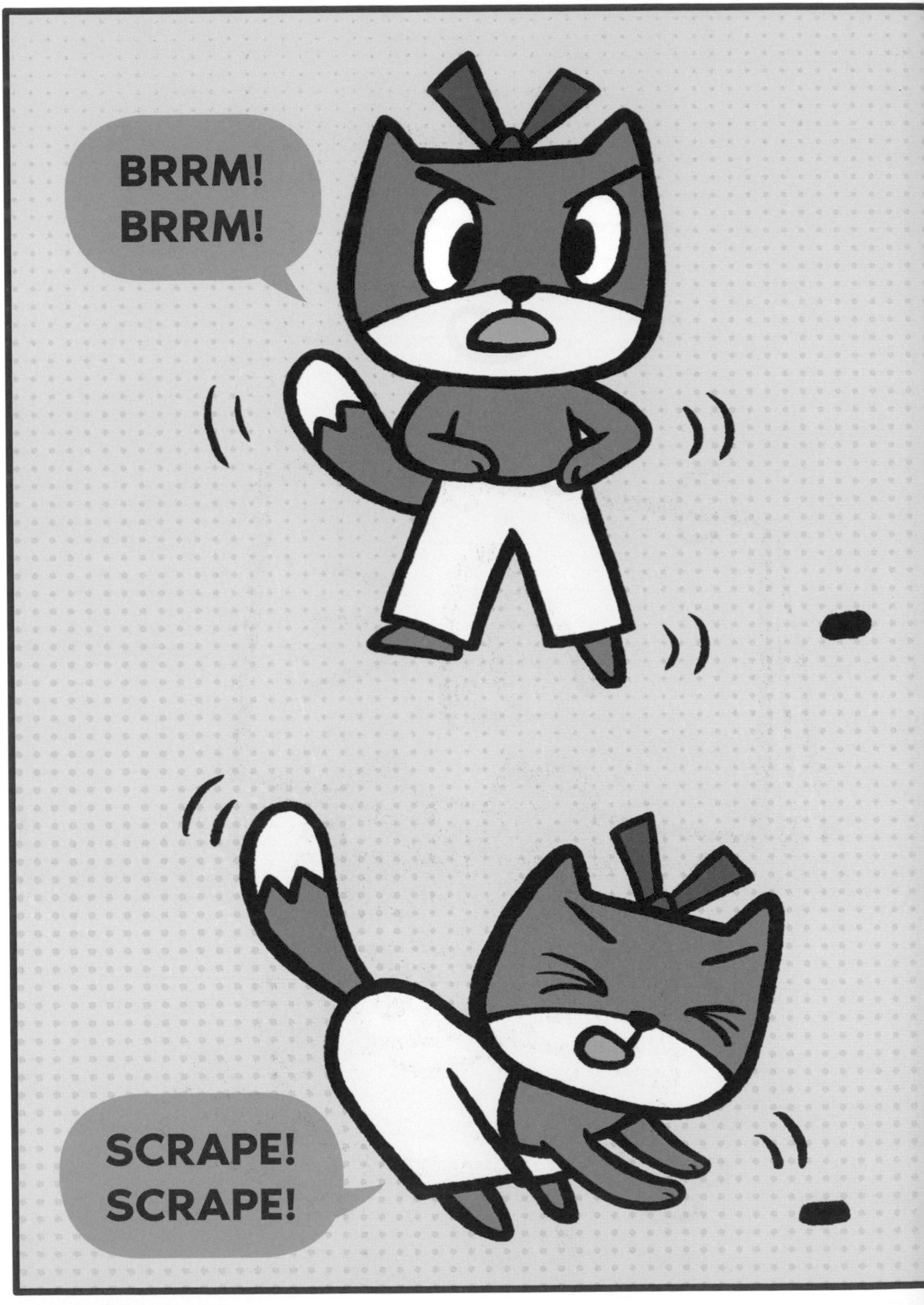
BRRM!
BRRM!
SCRAPE!
SCRAPE!

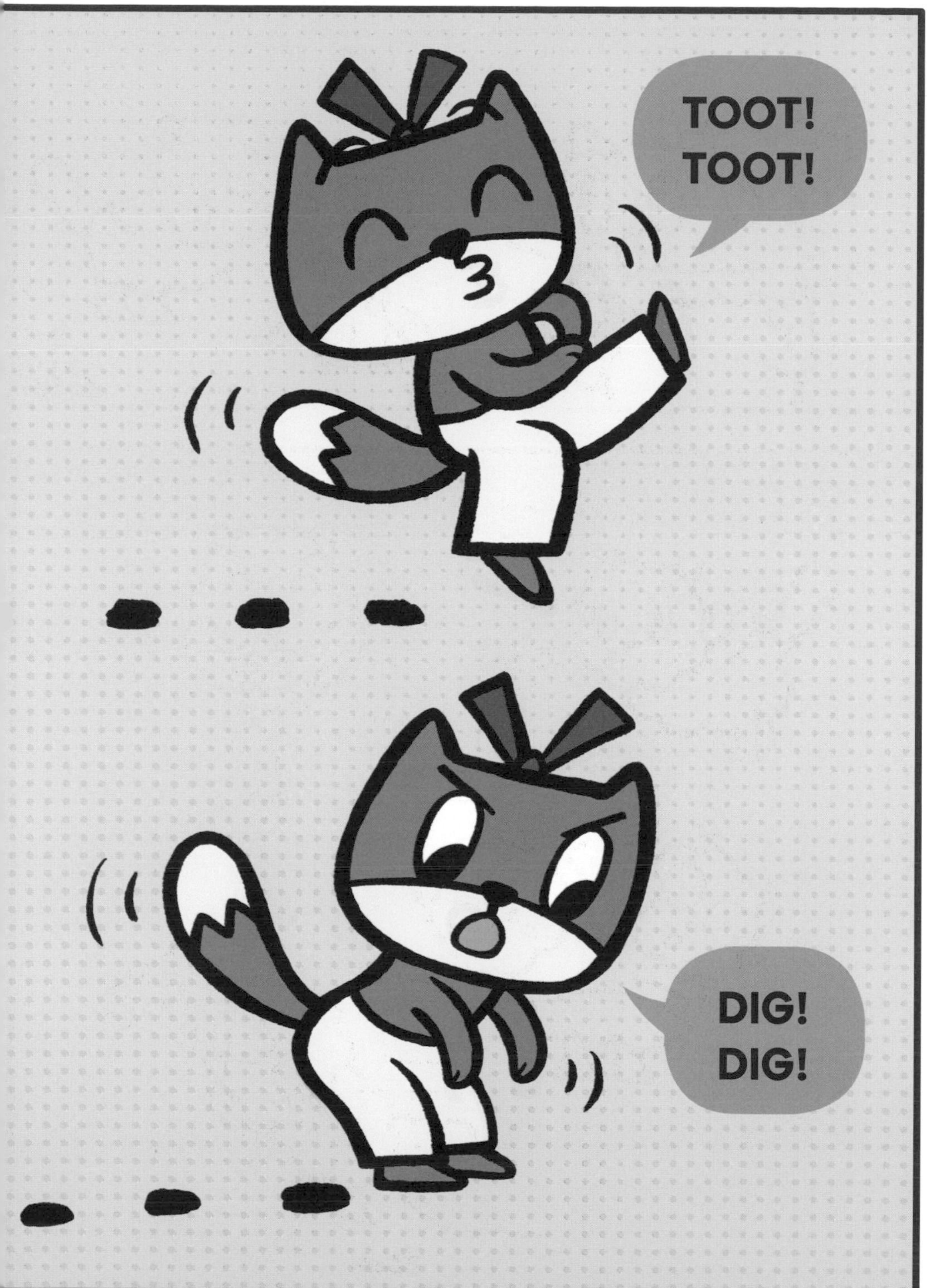
TOOT!
TOOT!
DIG!
DIG!

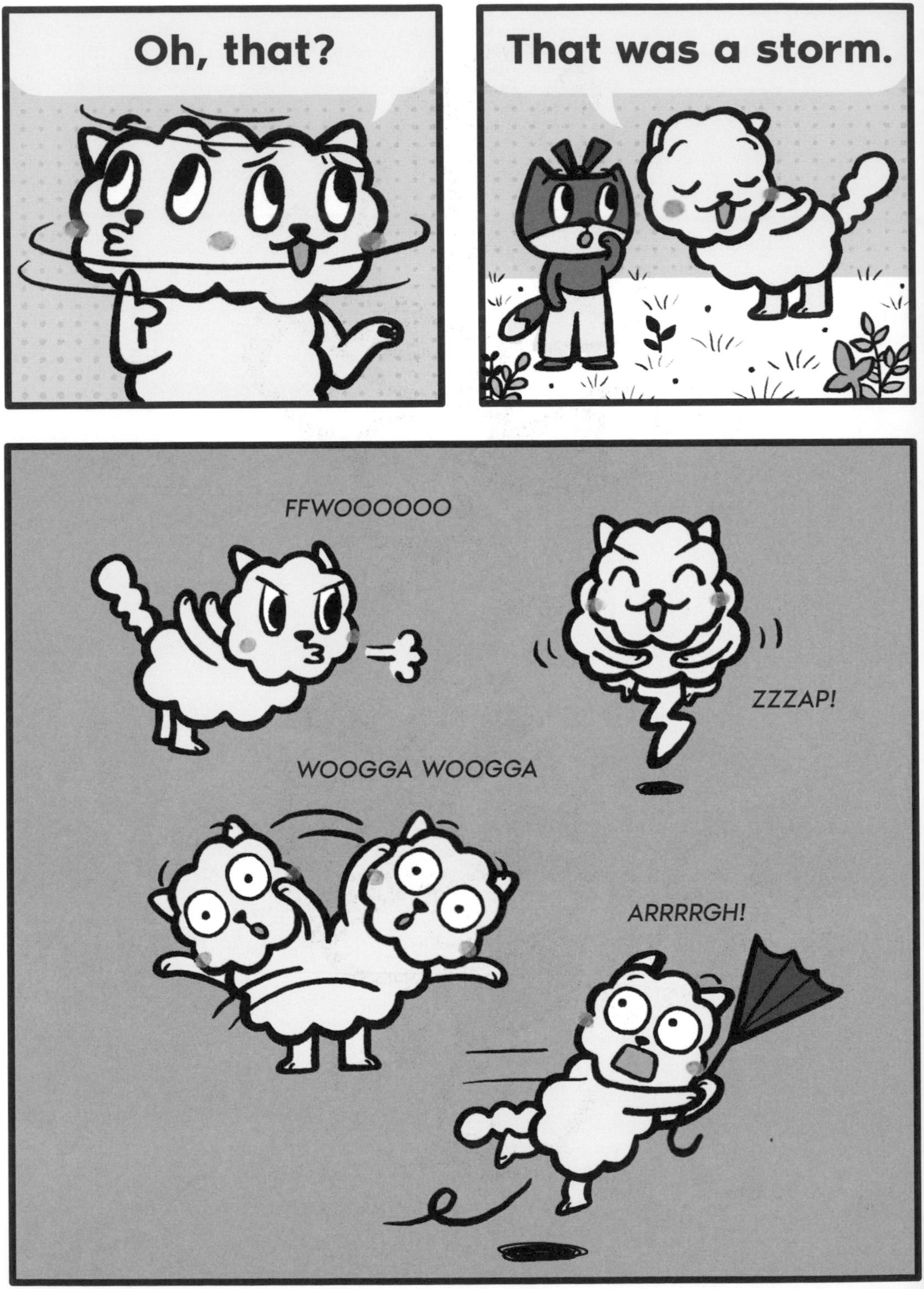
Oh, that?
That was a storm.
FFWOOOOOO
ZZZAP!
WOOGGA WOOGGA
ARRRRGH!

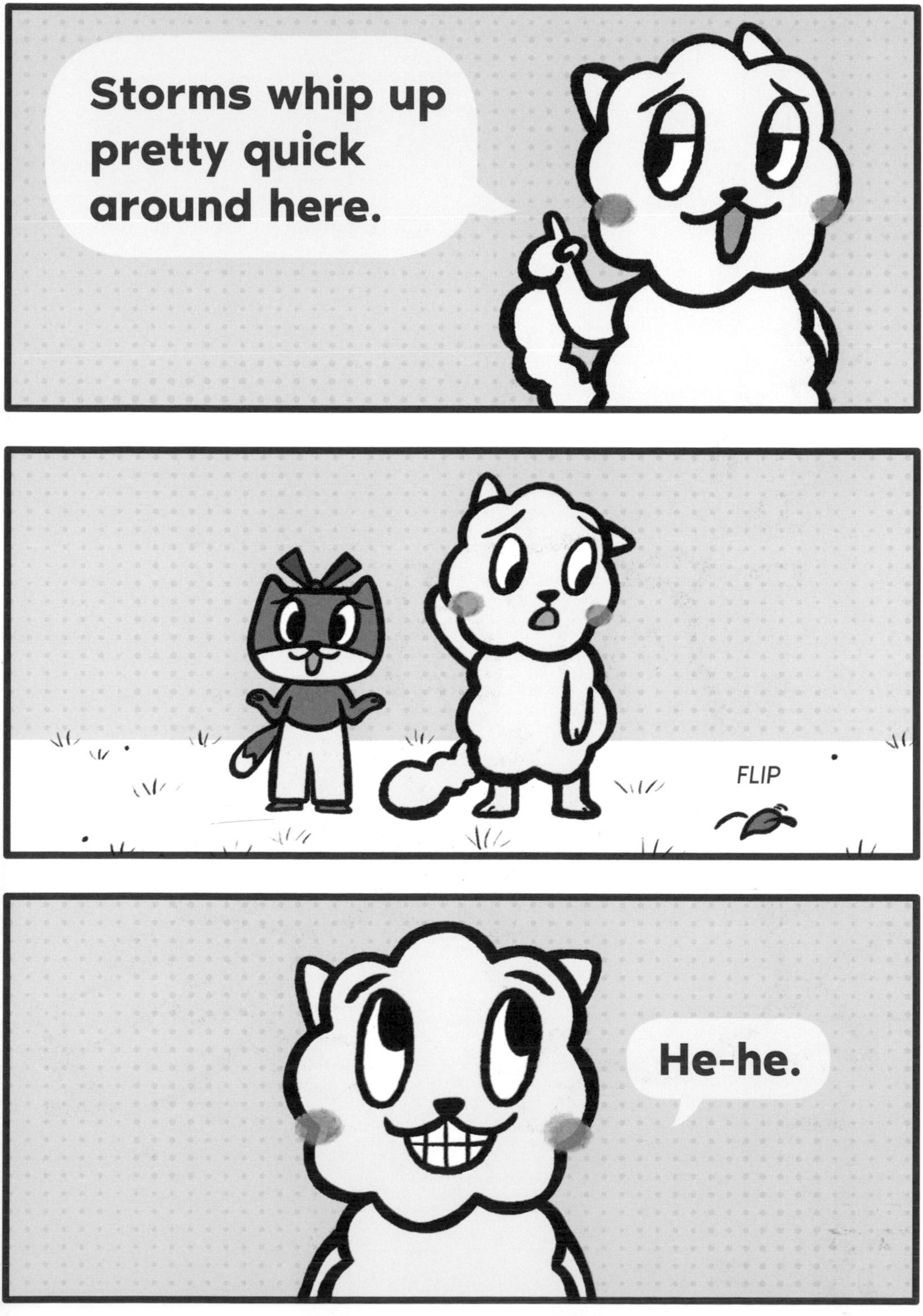
Storms whip up pretty quick around here.
FLIP
He-he.

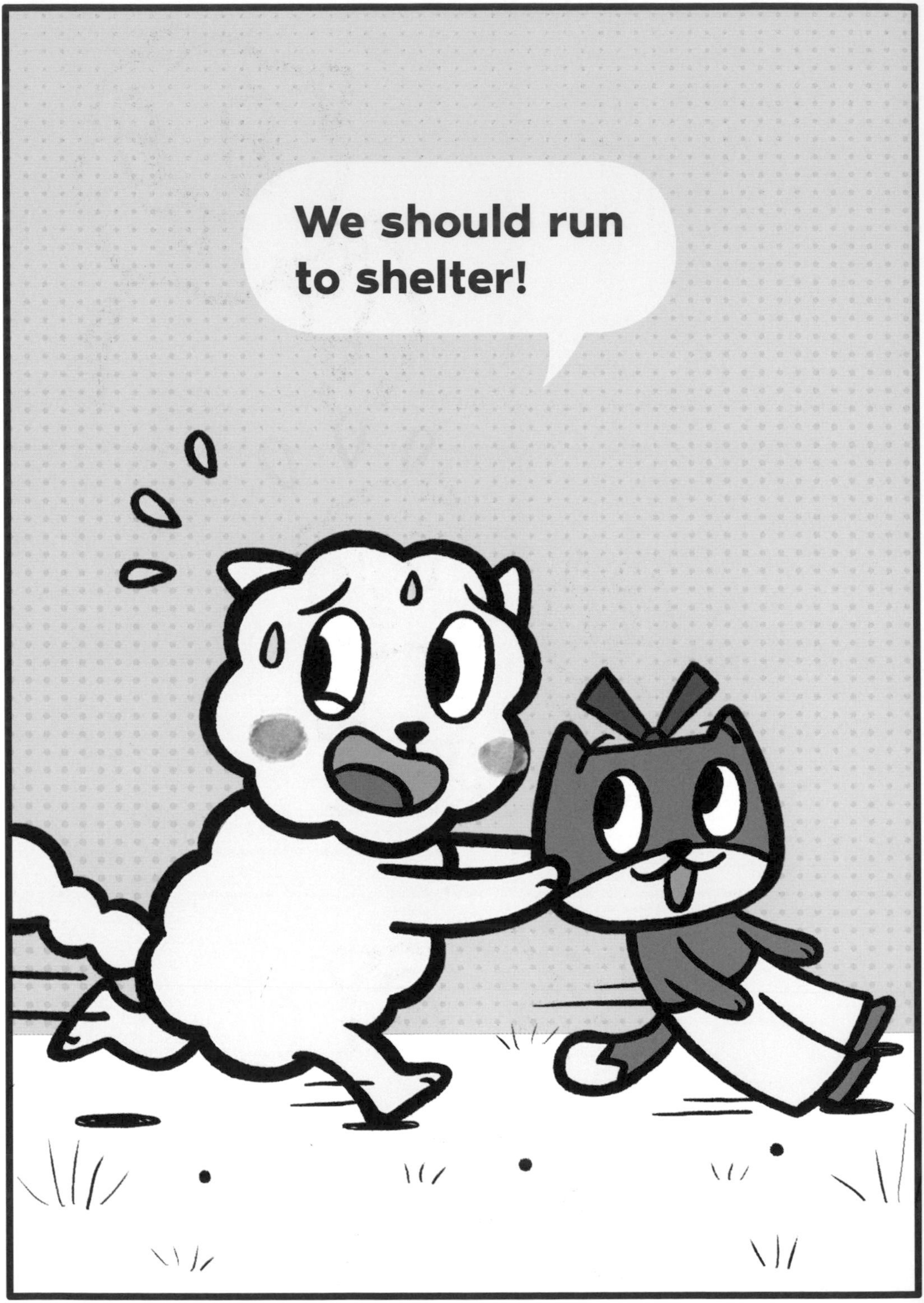
We should run to shelter!

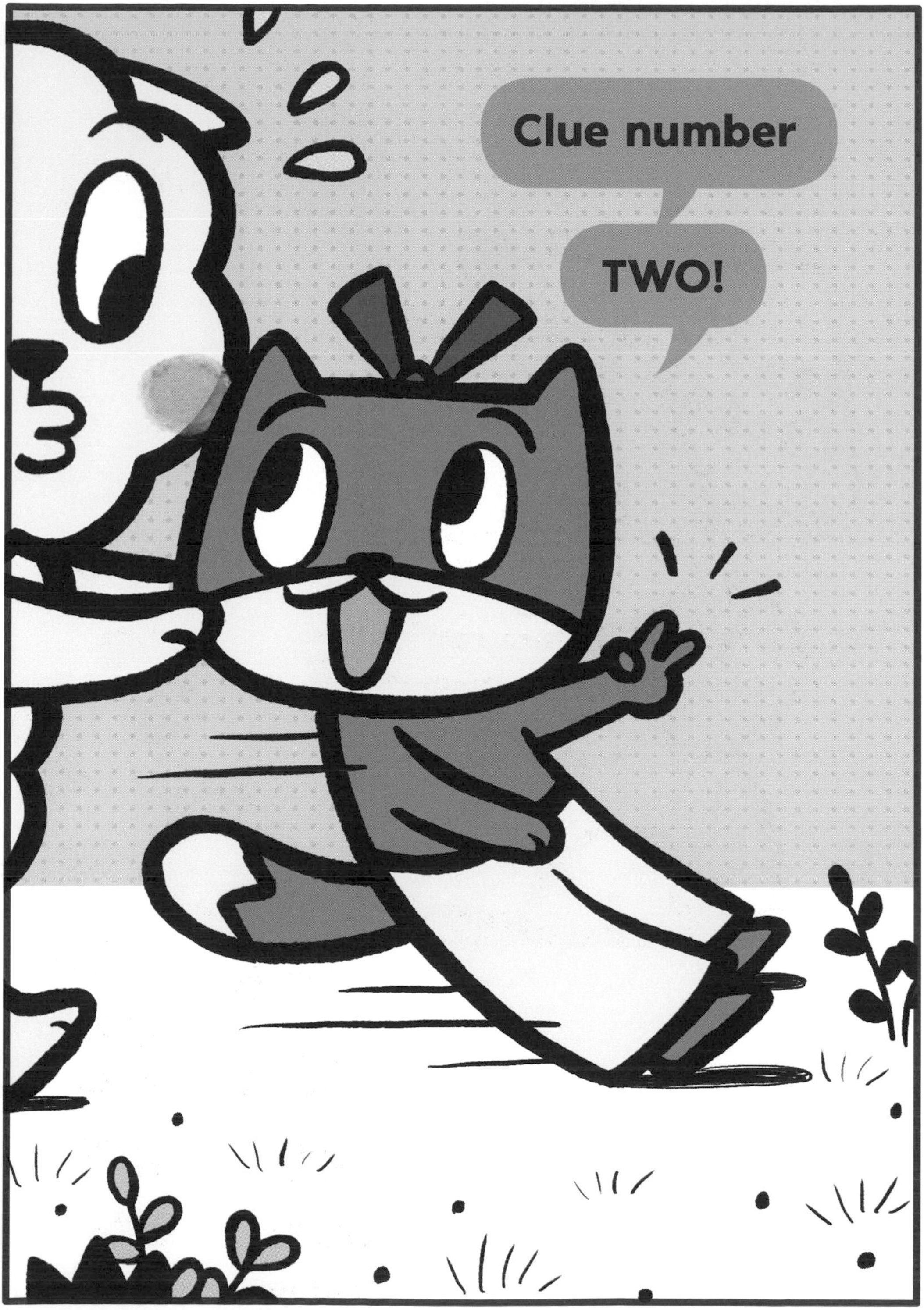
Clue number
TWO!

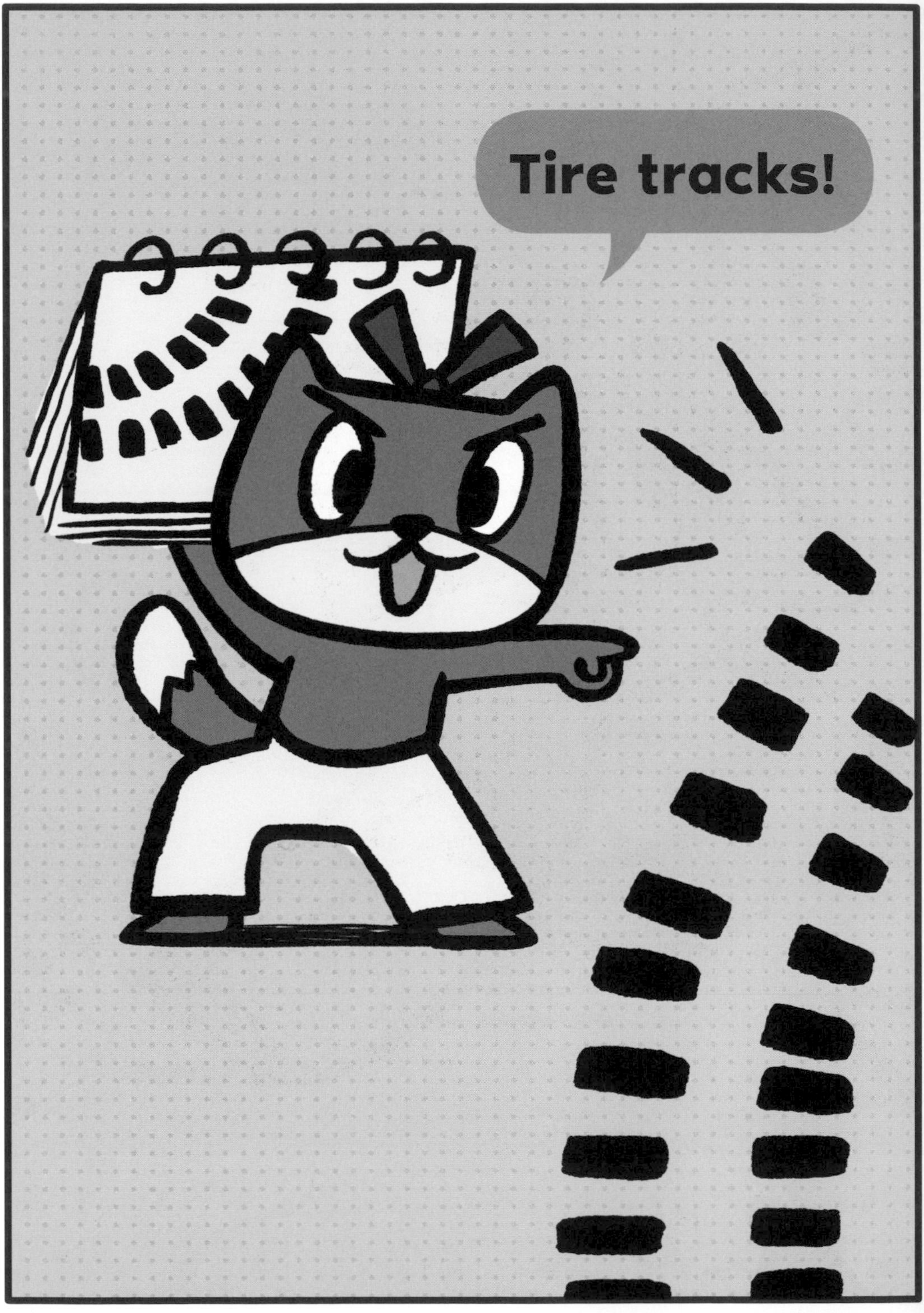
Tire tracks!

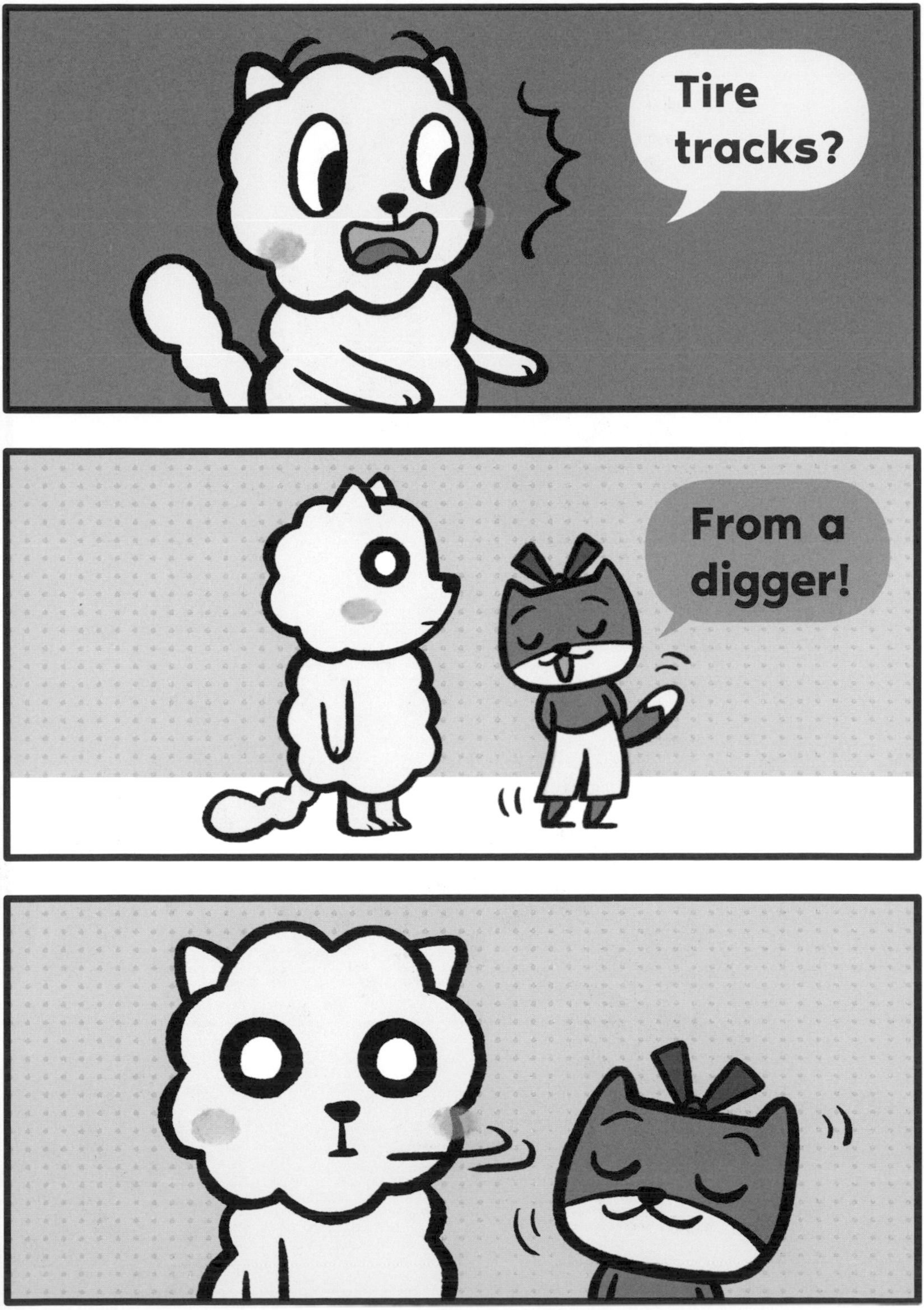
Tire tracks?
From a digger!

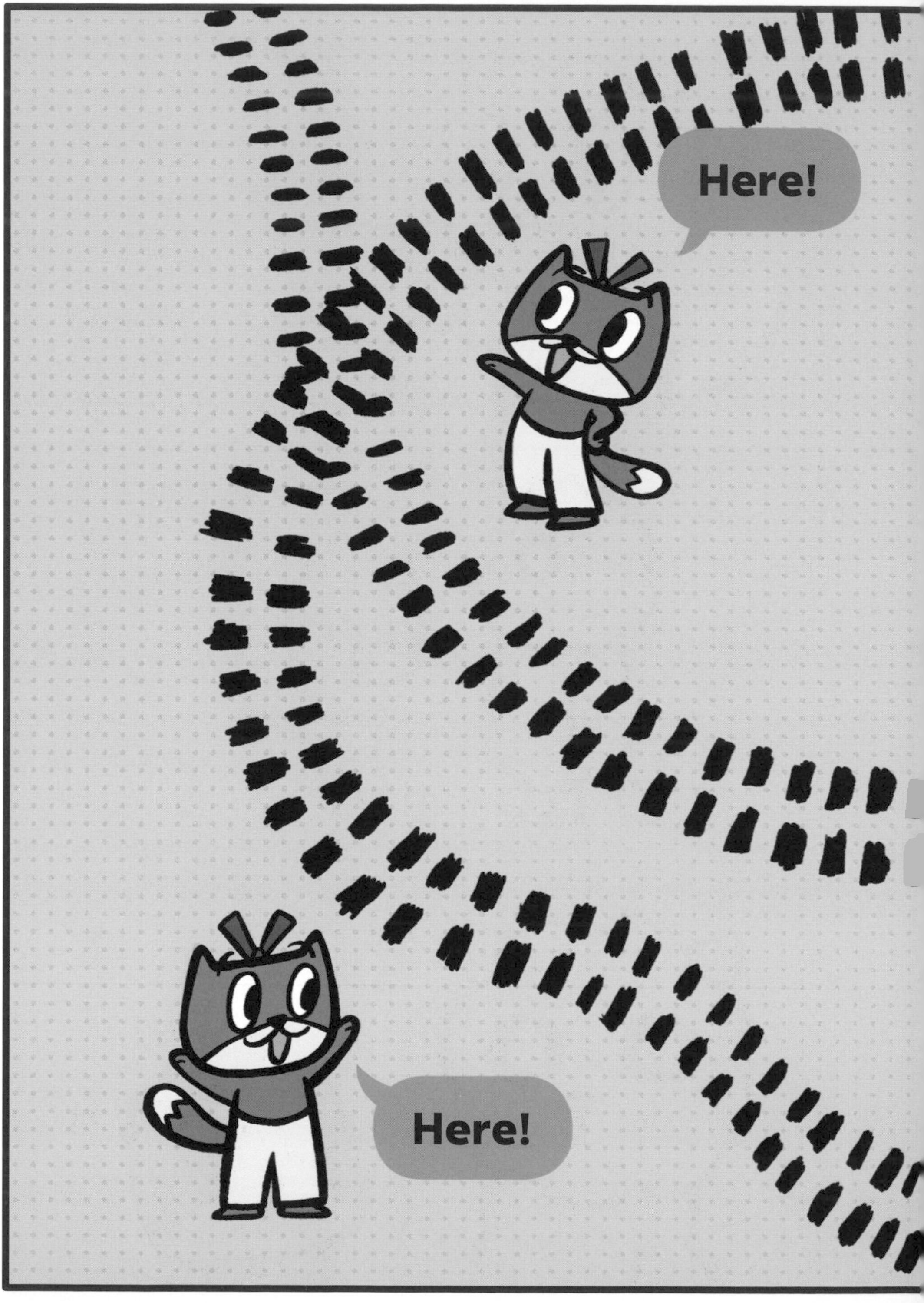
Here!
Here!

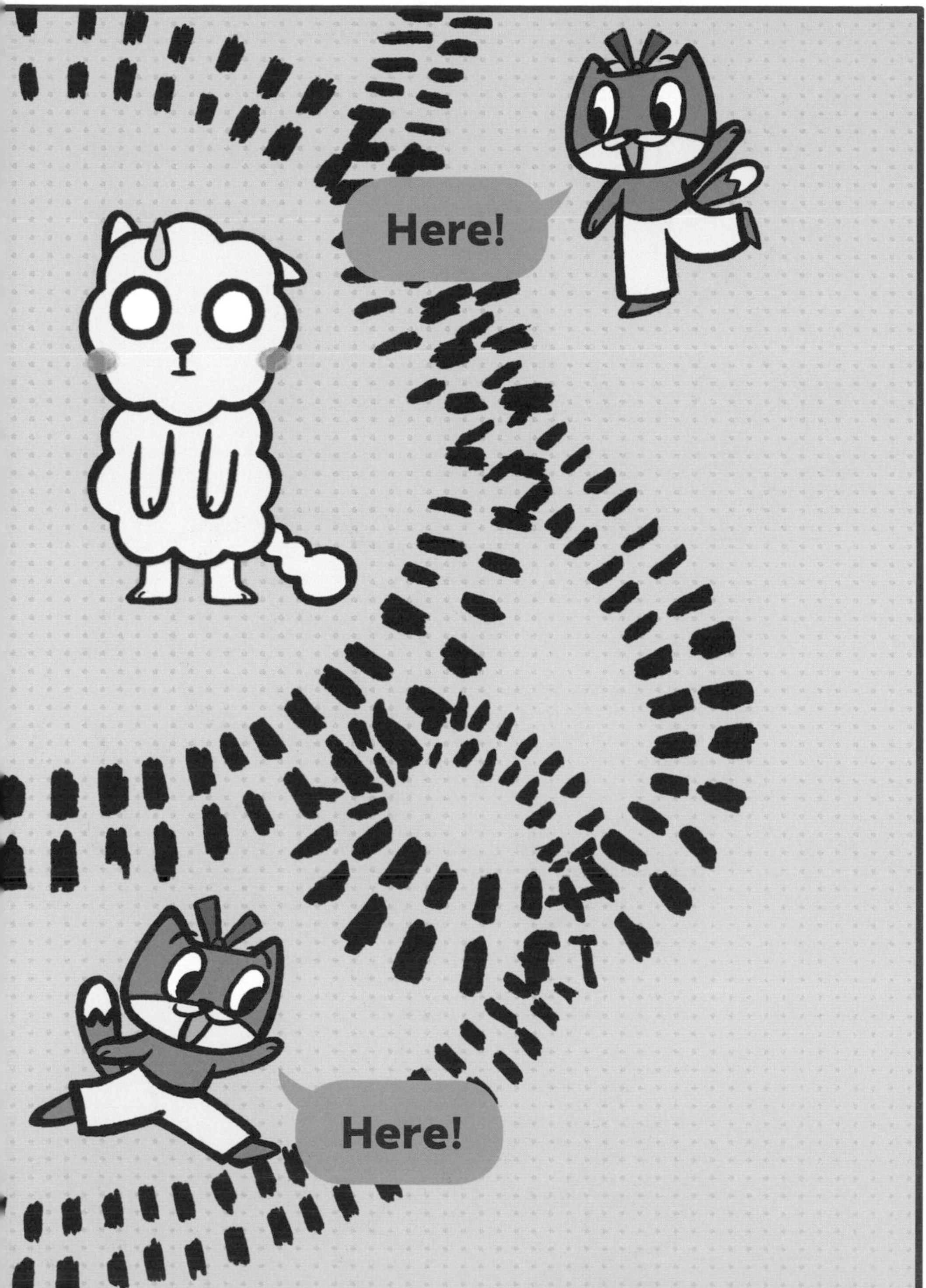
Here!
Here!

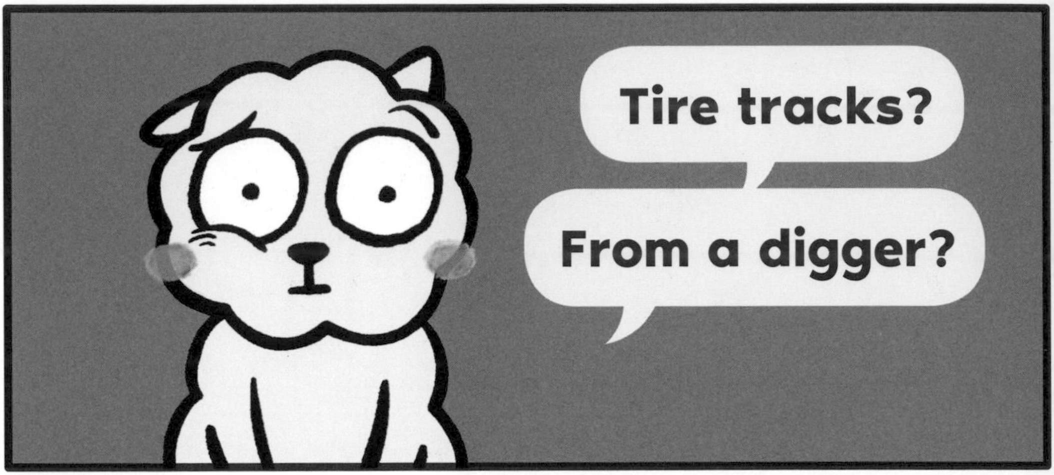
Tire tracks?
From a digger?

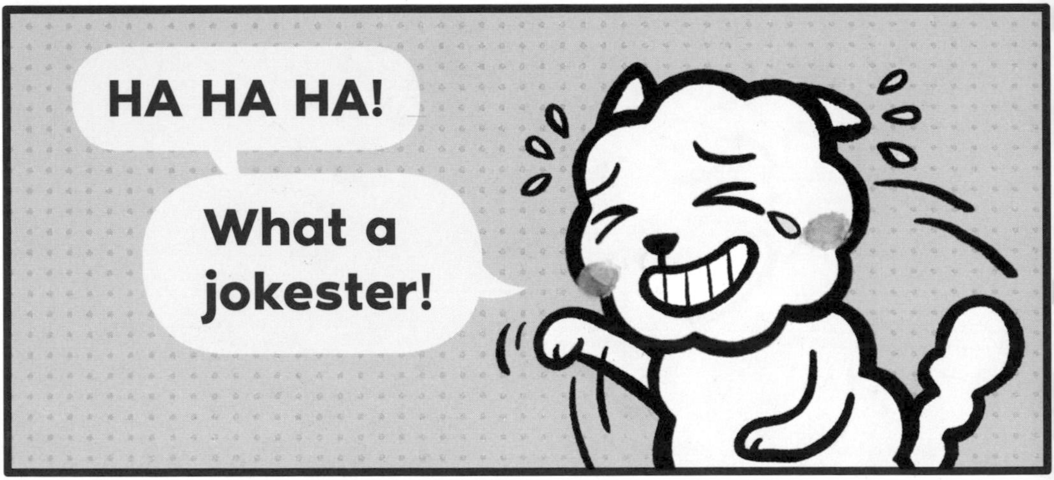
HA HA HA!
What a jokester!

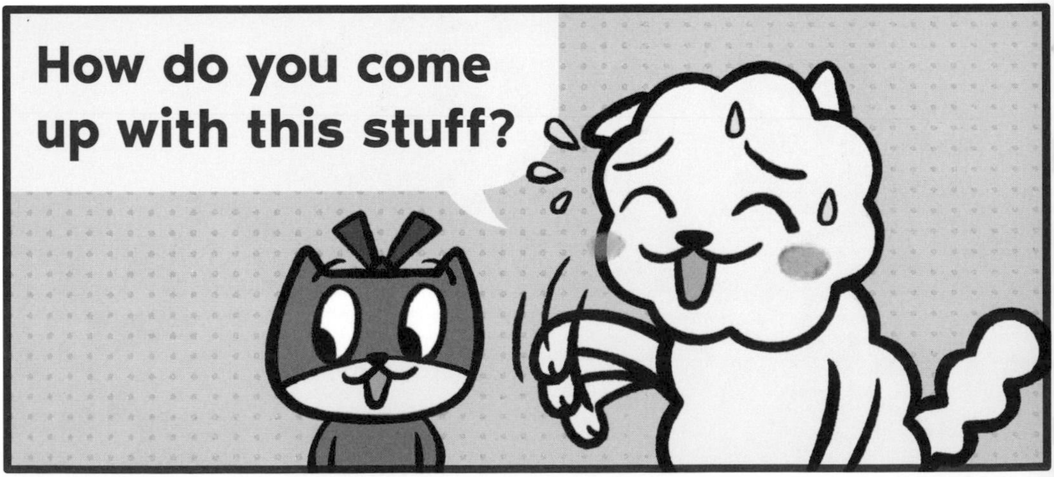
How do you come up with this stuff?

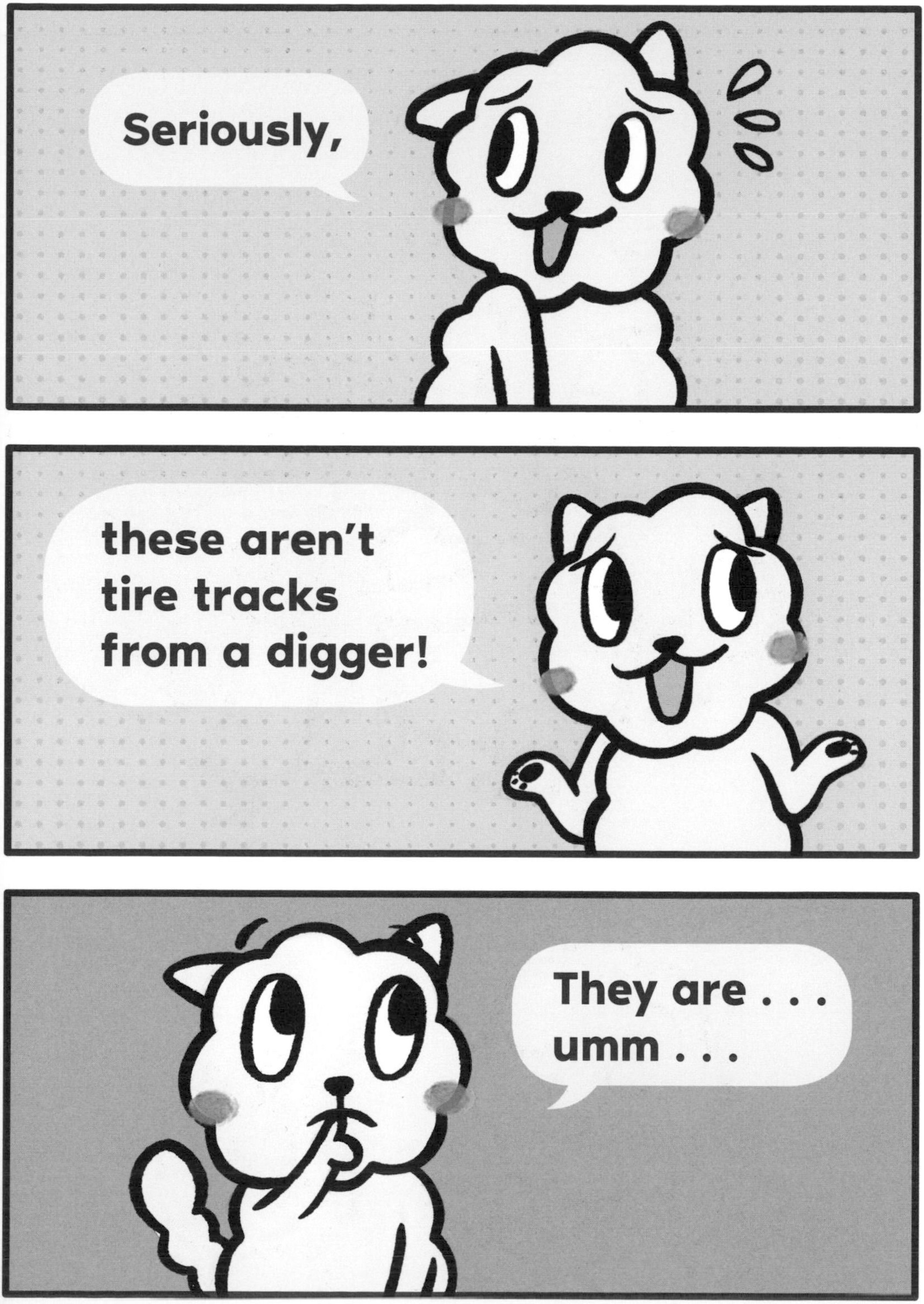
Seriously,
these aren't tire tracks from a digger!
They are . . . umm . . .

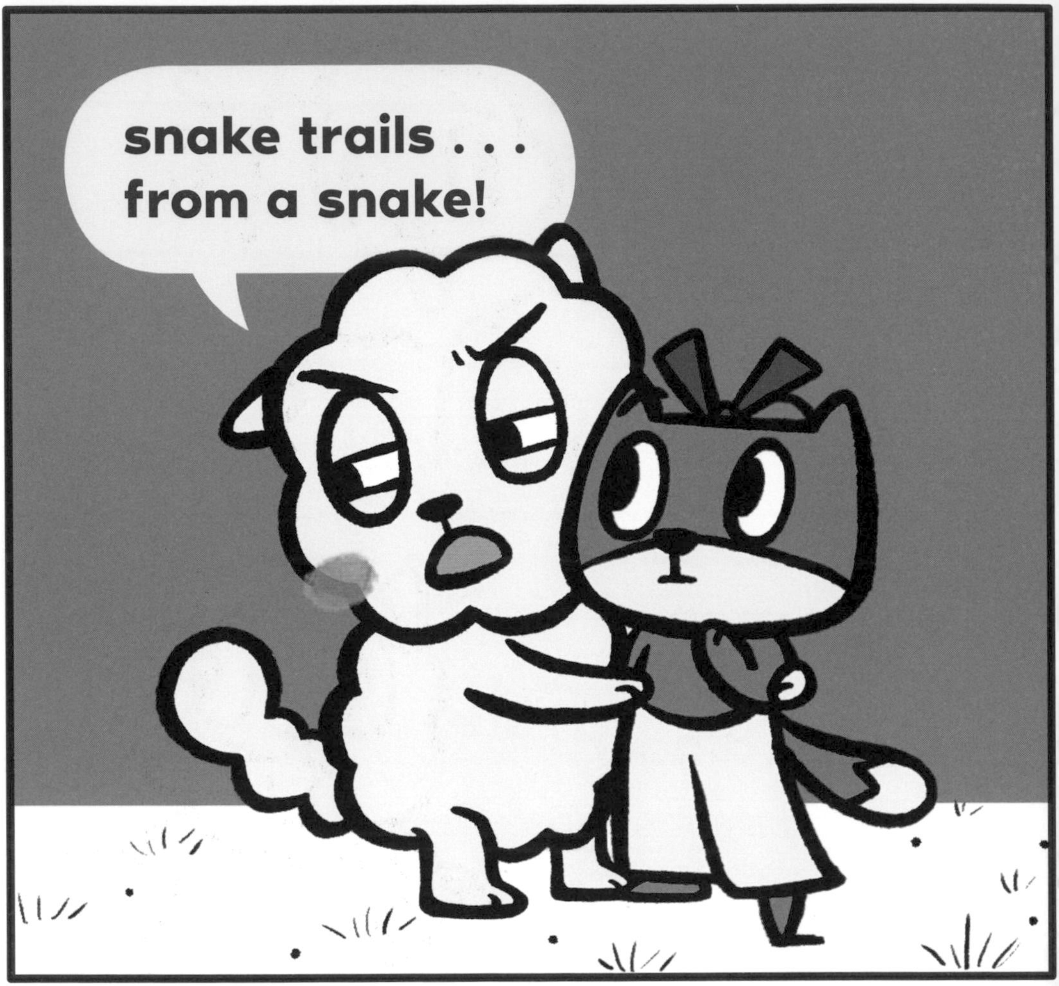
snake trails . . .
from a snake!

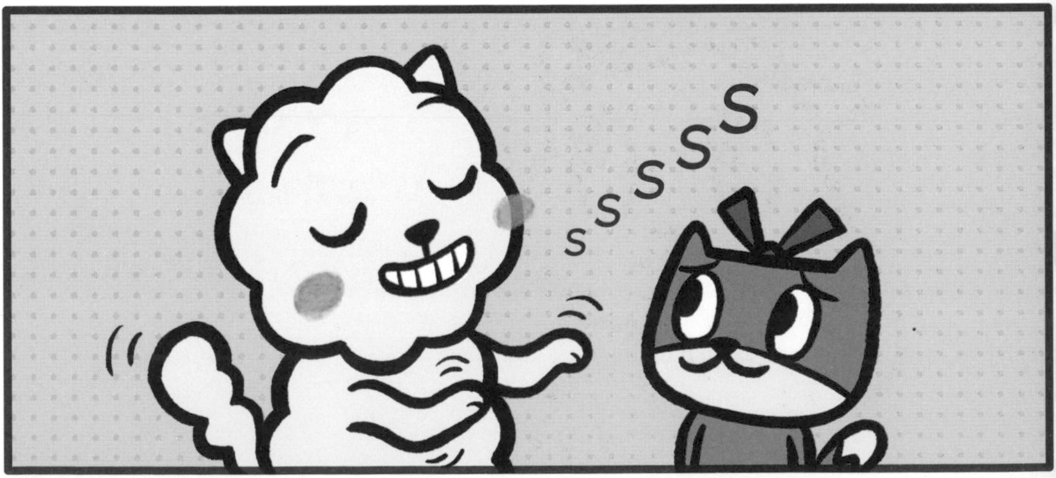
SSSSSSS

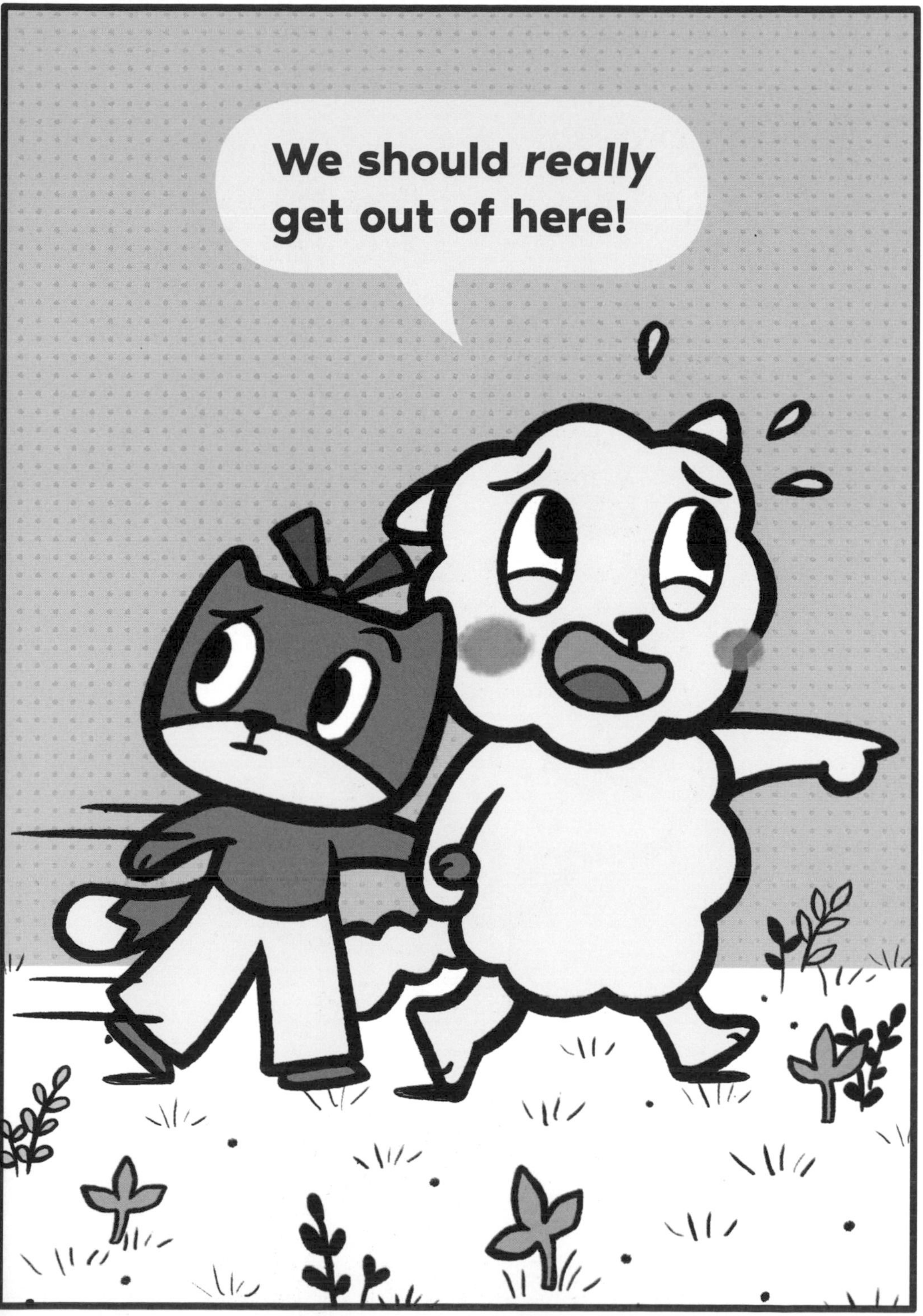
We should *really* get out of here!

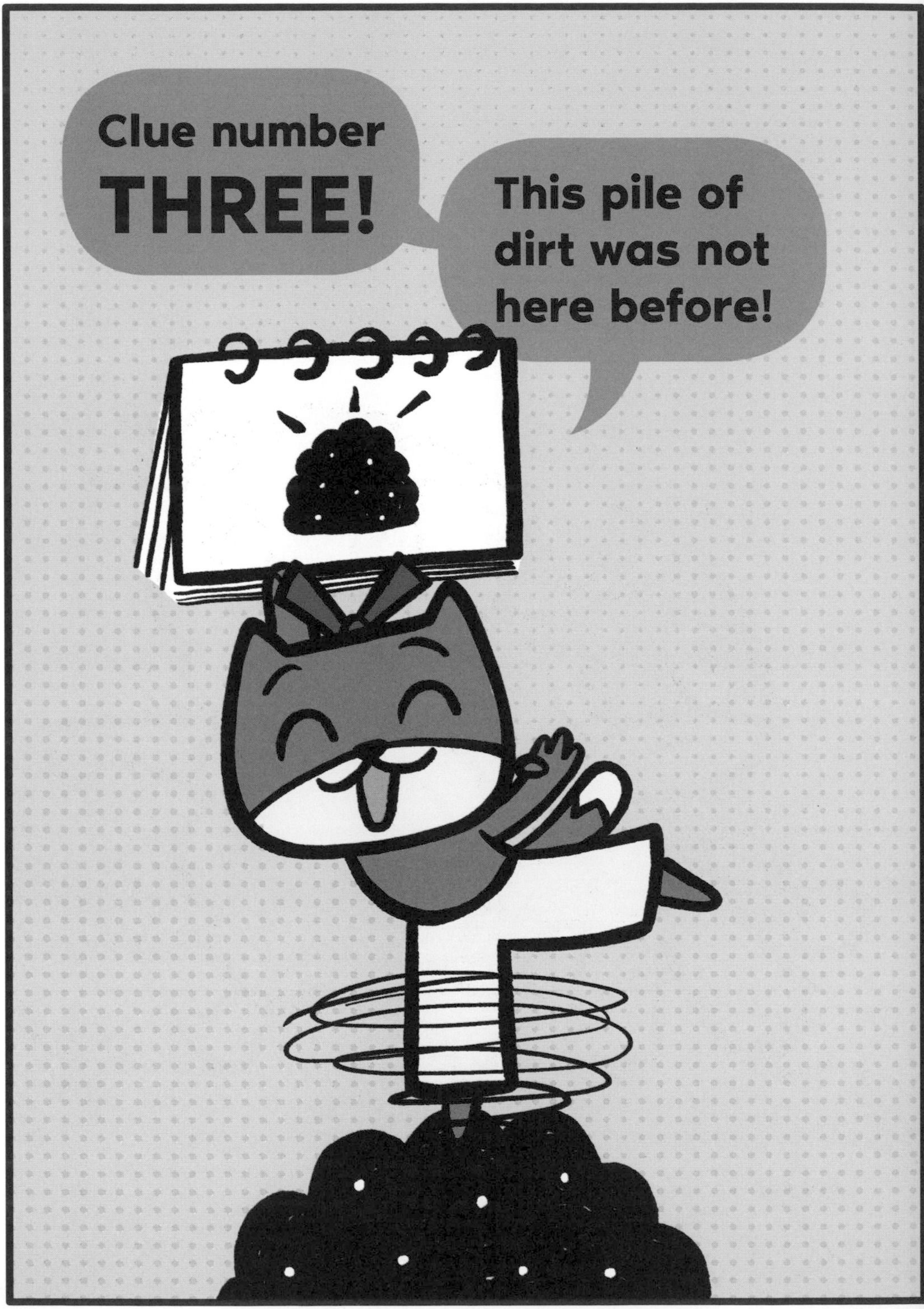
Clue number THREE!
This pile of dirt was not here before!

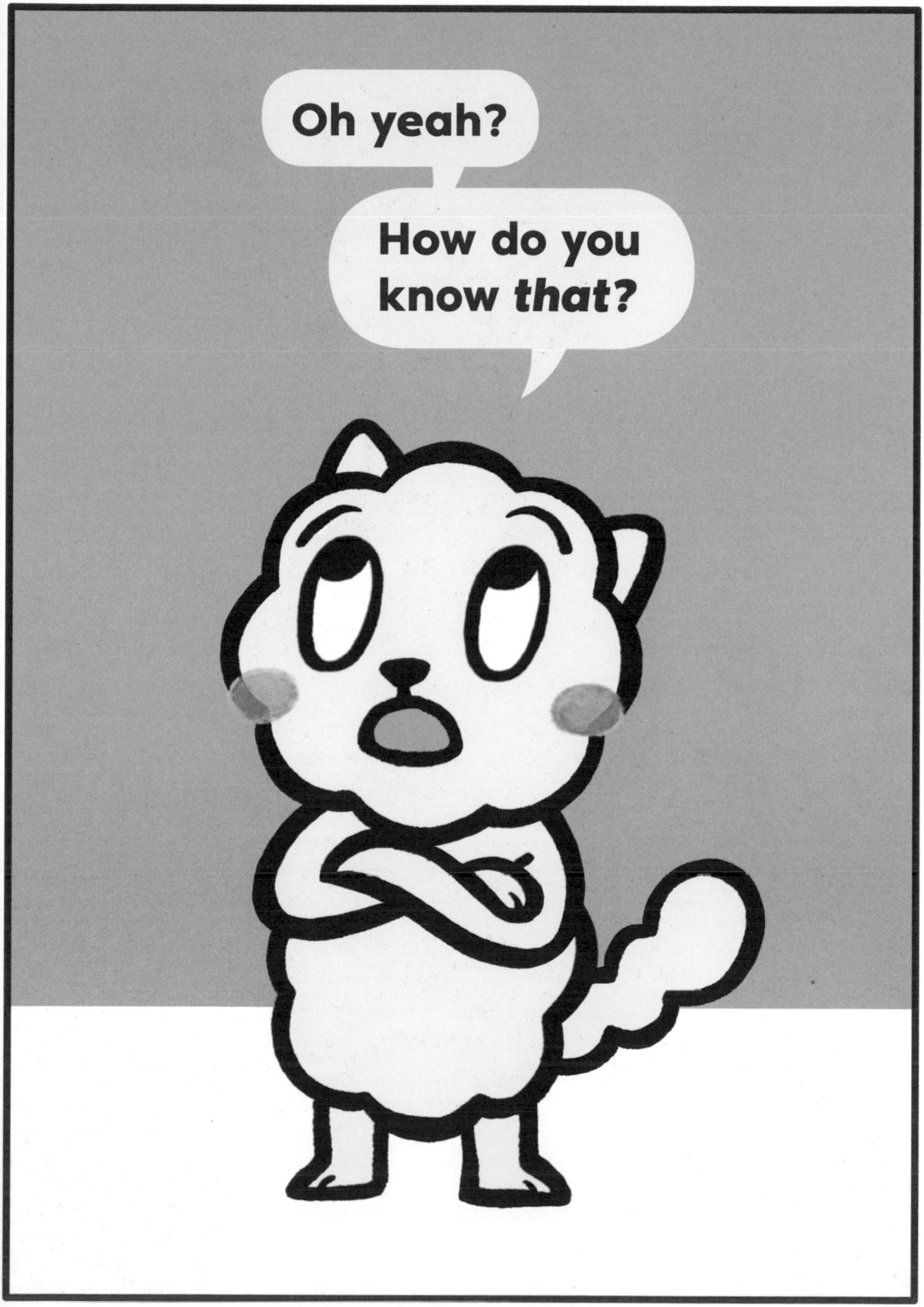
Oh yeah?
How do you know *that*?

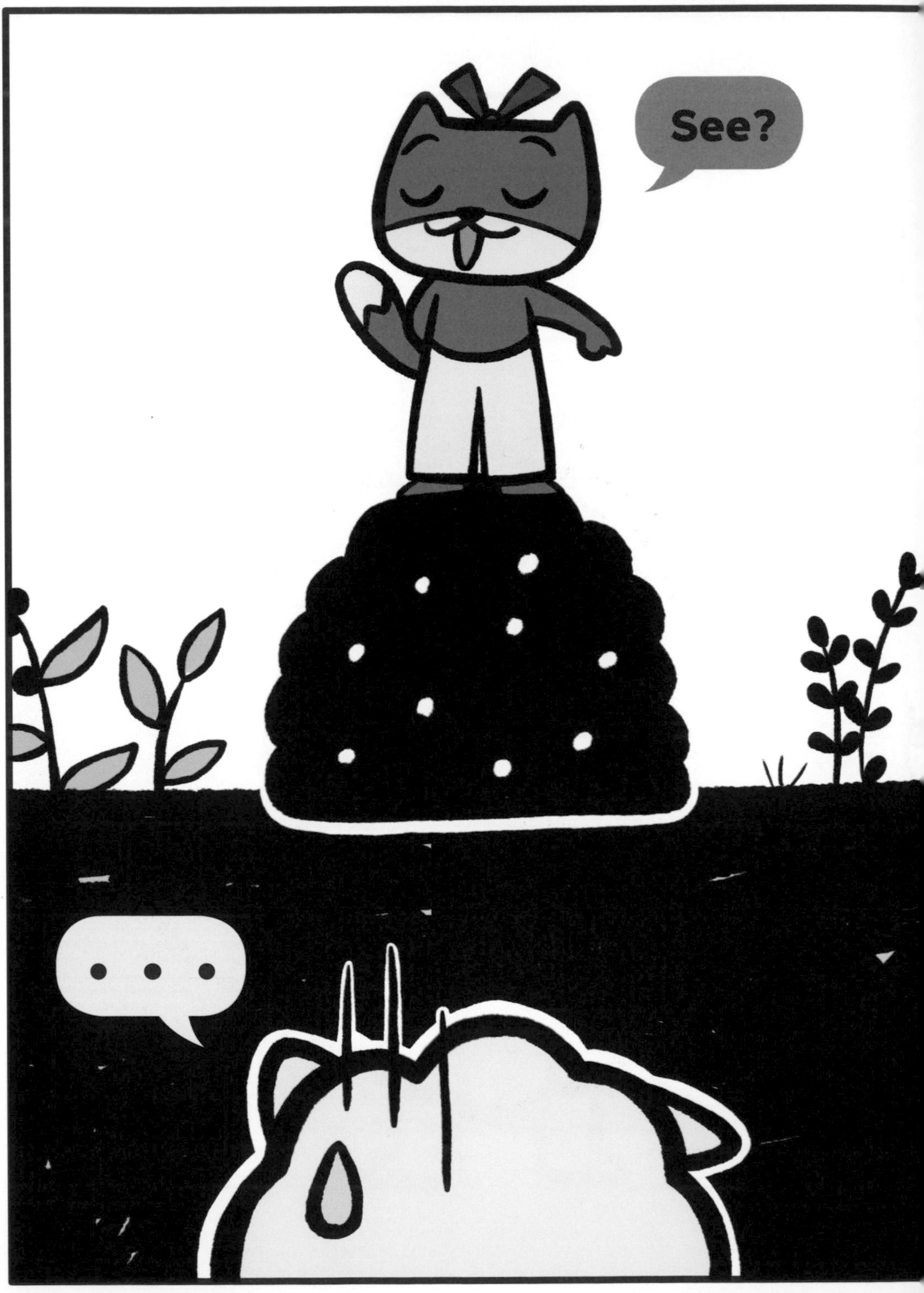
See?
...

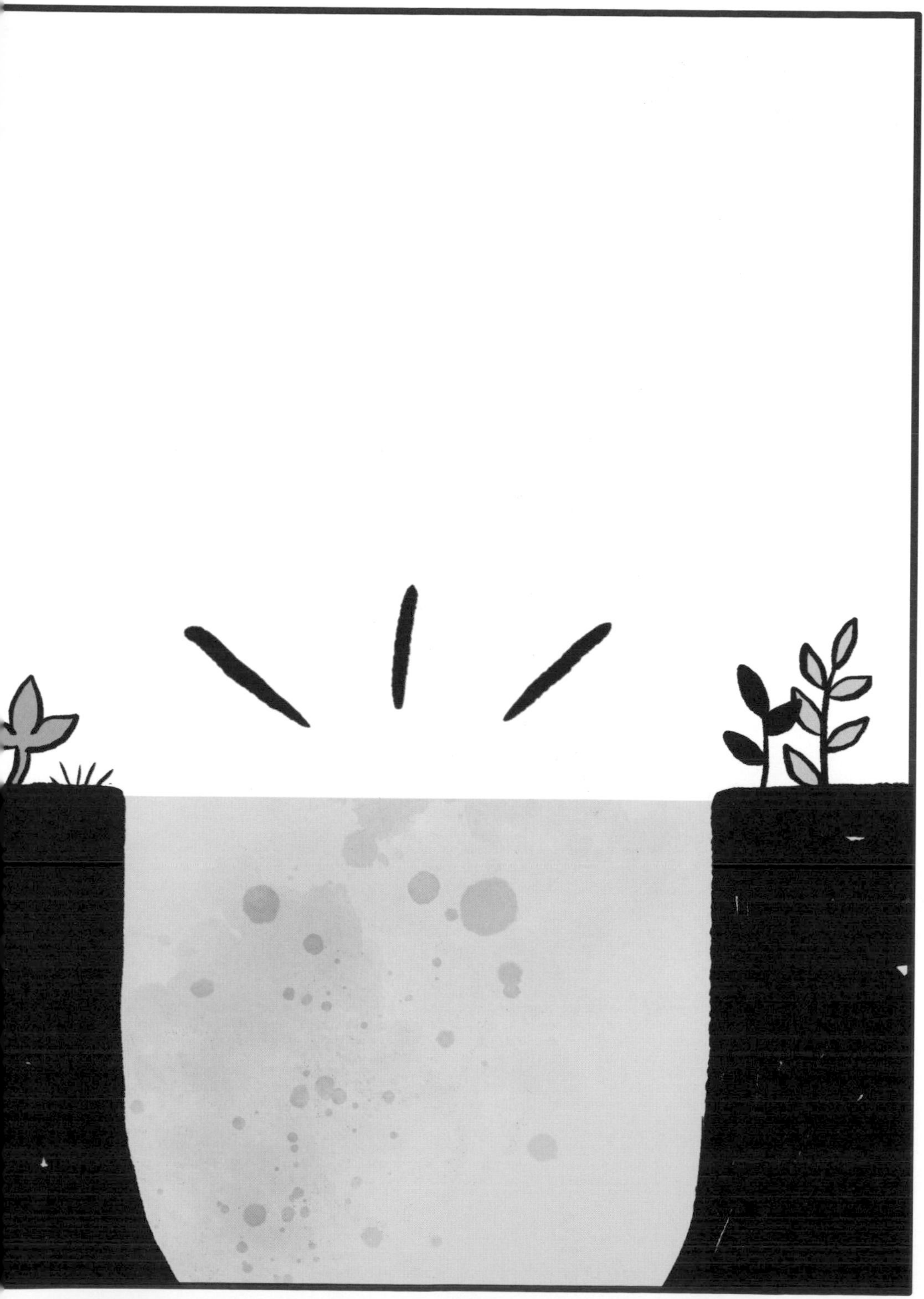

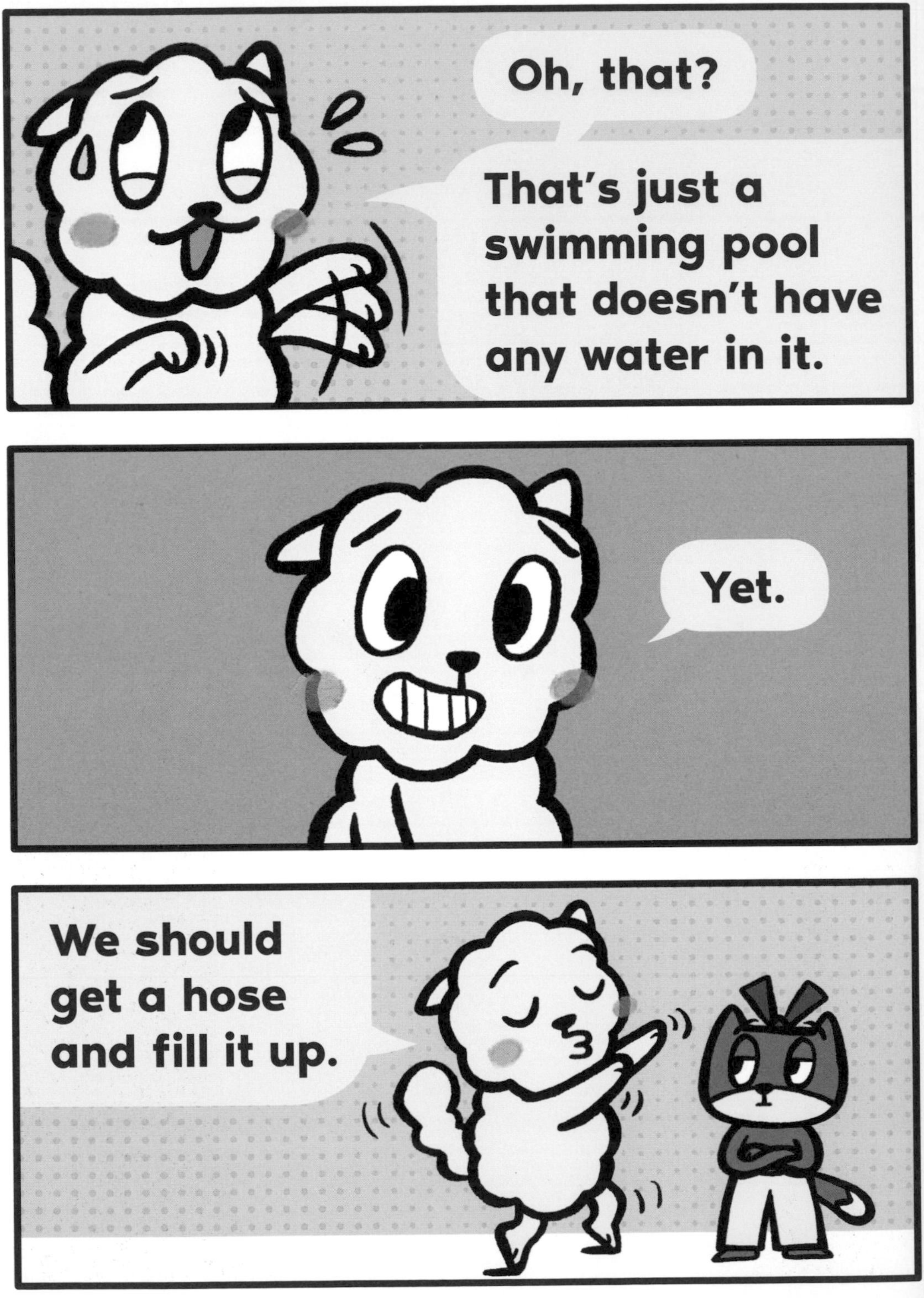
Oh, that?
That's just a swimming pool that doesn't have any water in it.
Yet.
We should get a hose and fill it up.

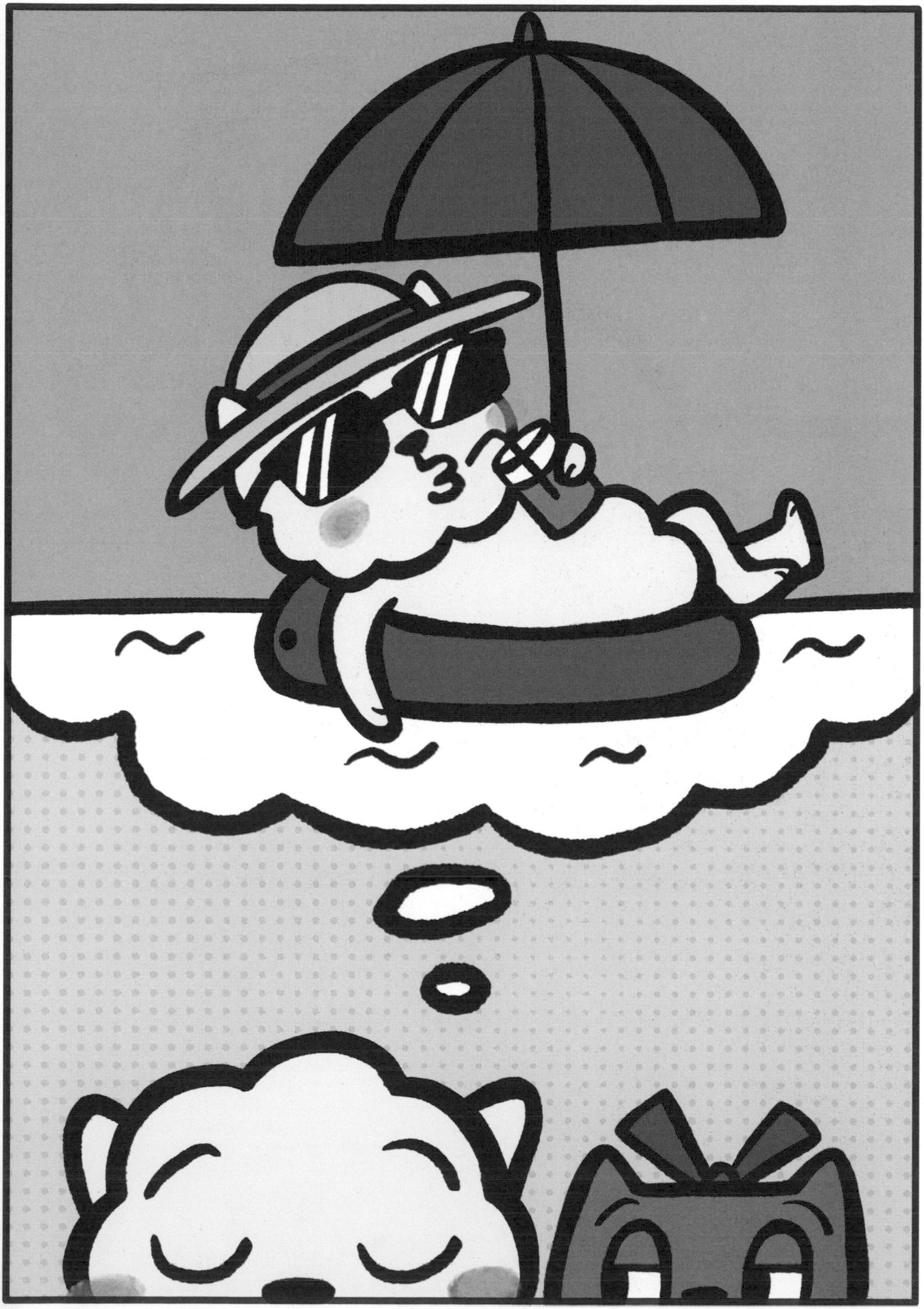

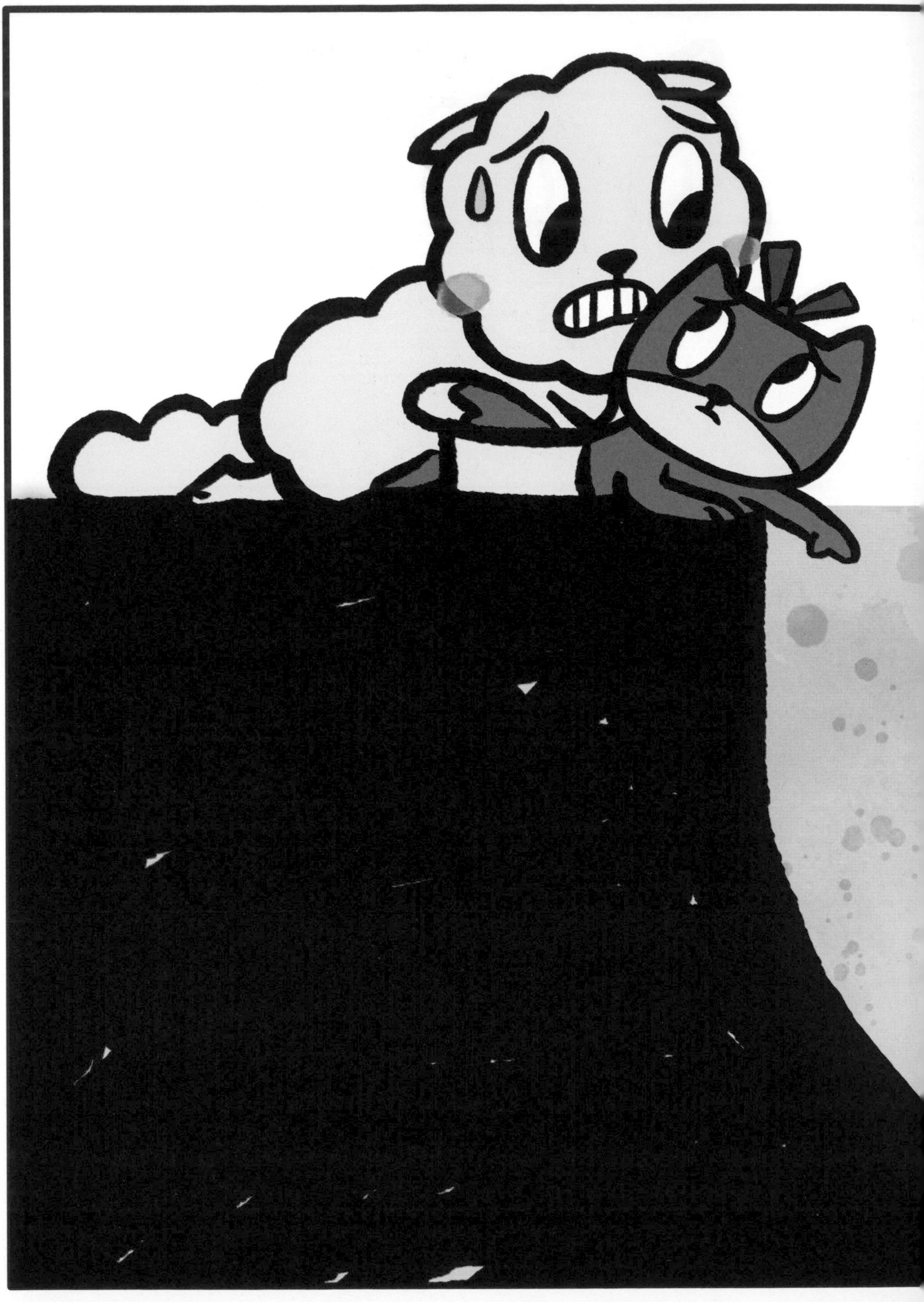

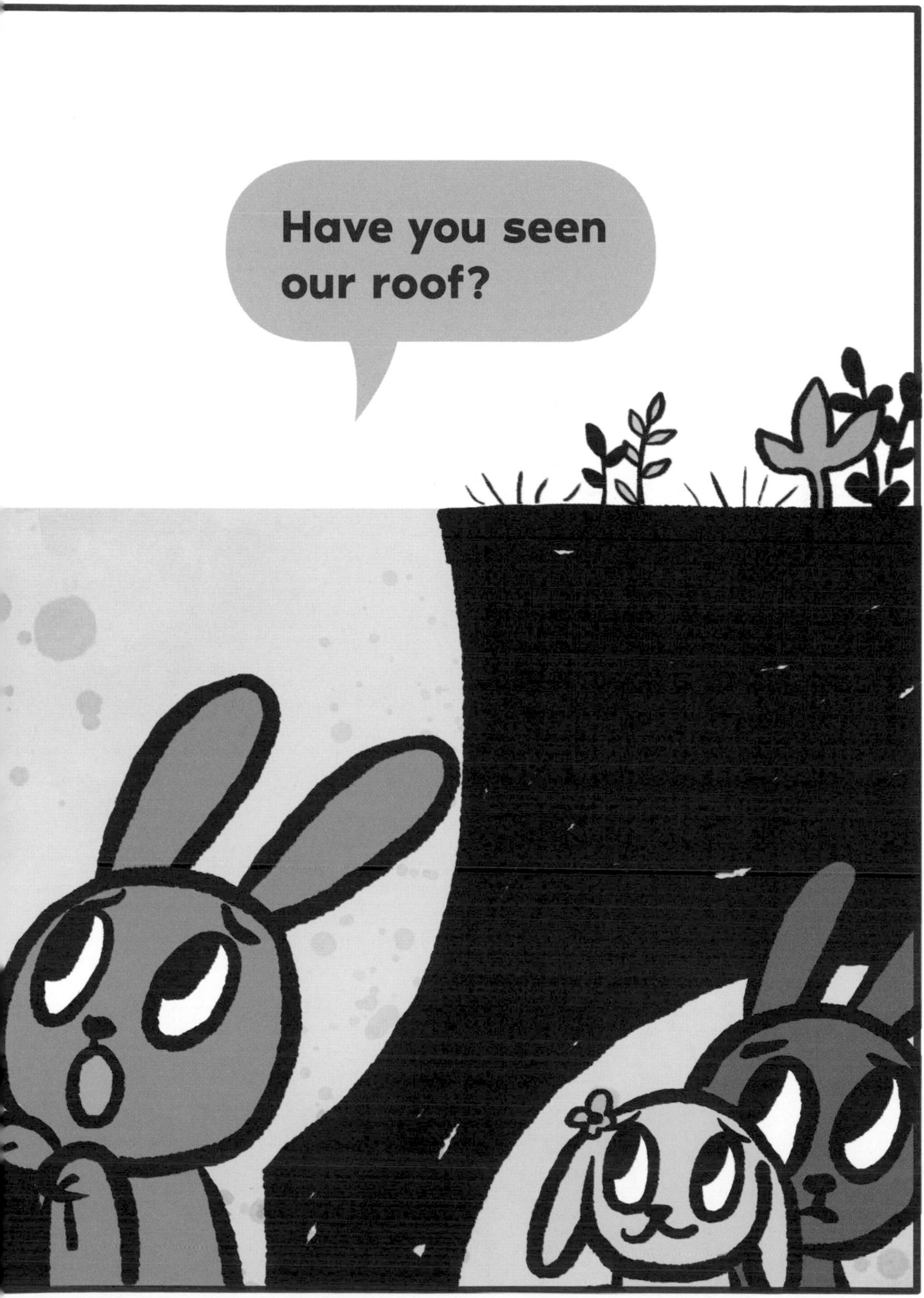
Have you seen our roof?

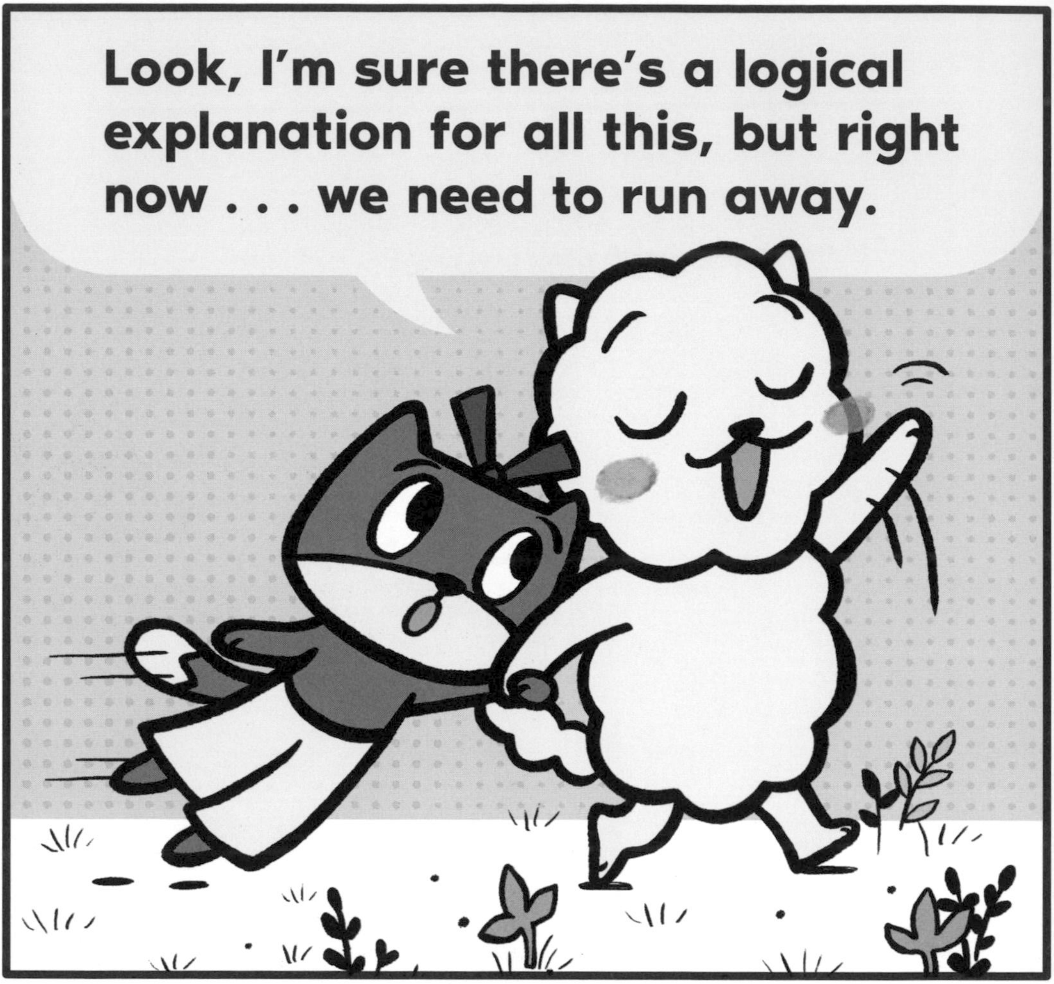
Look, I'm sure there's a logical explanation for all this, but right now . . . we need to run away.

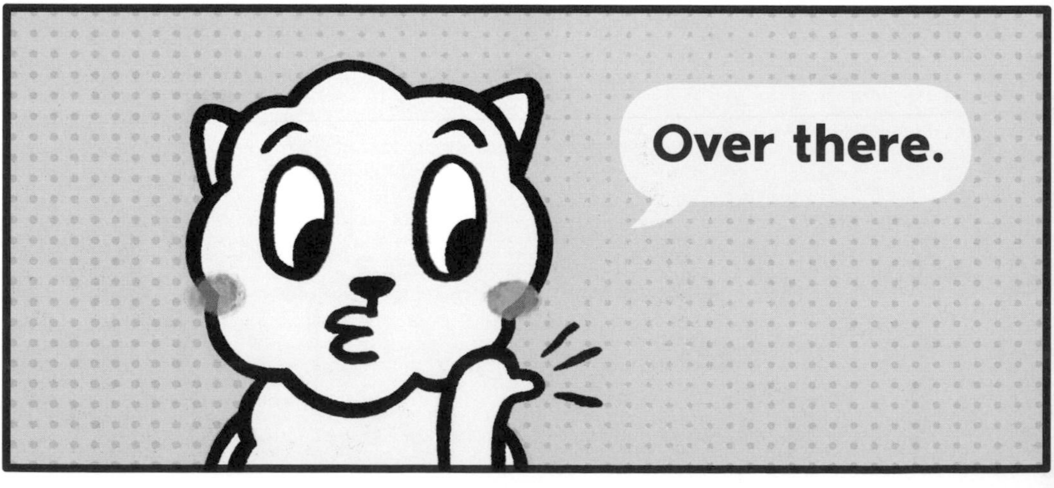
Over there.

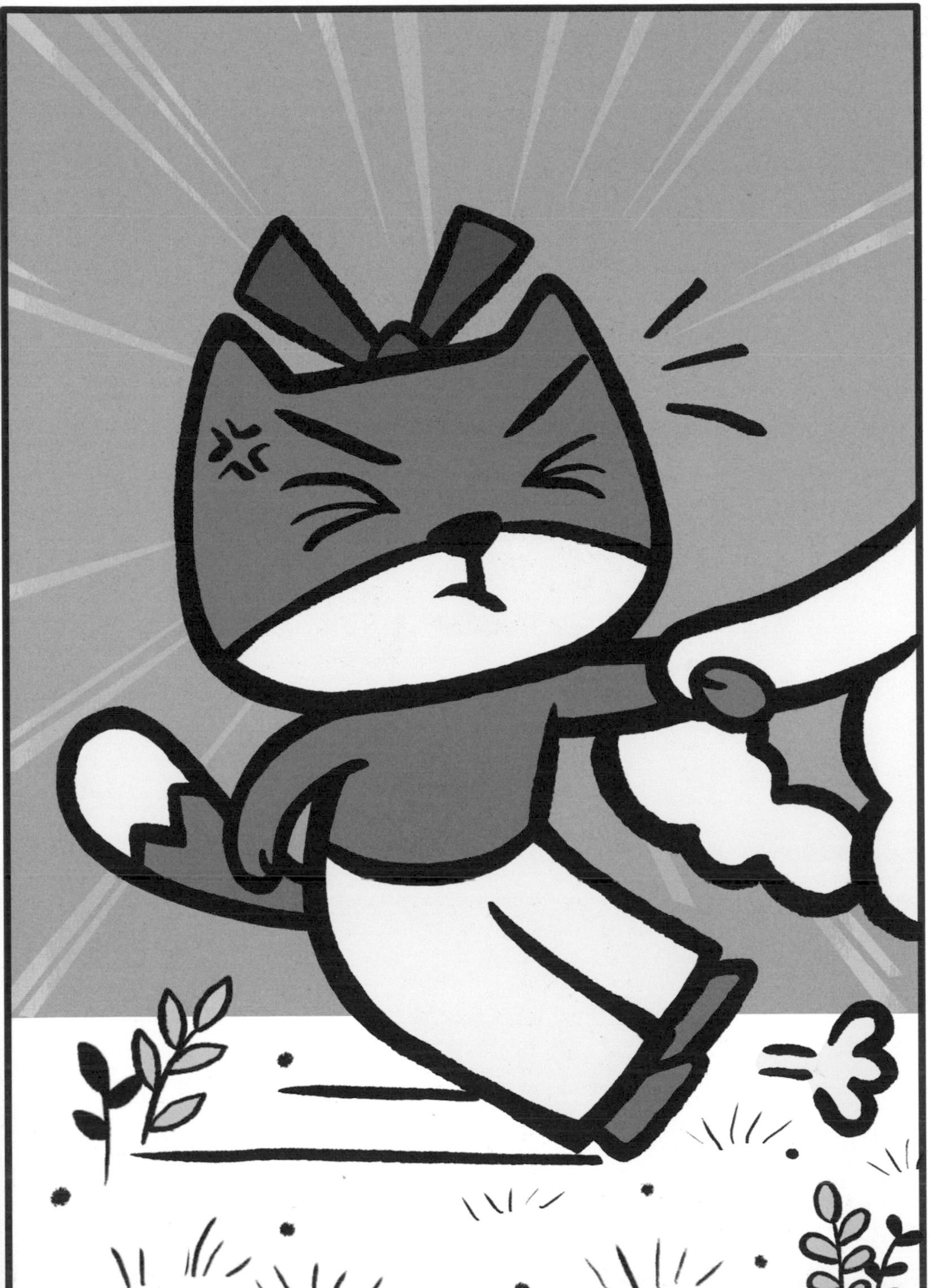

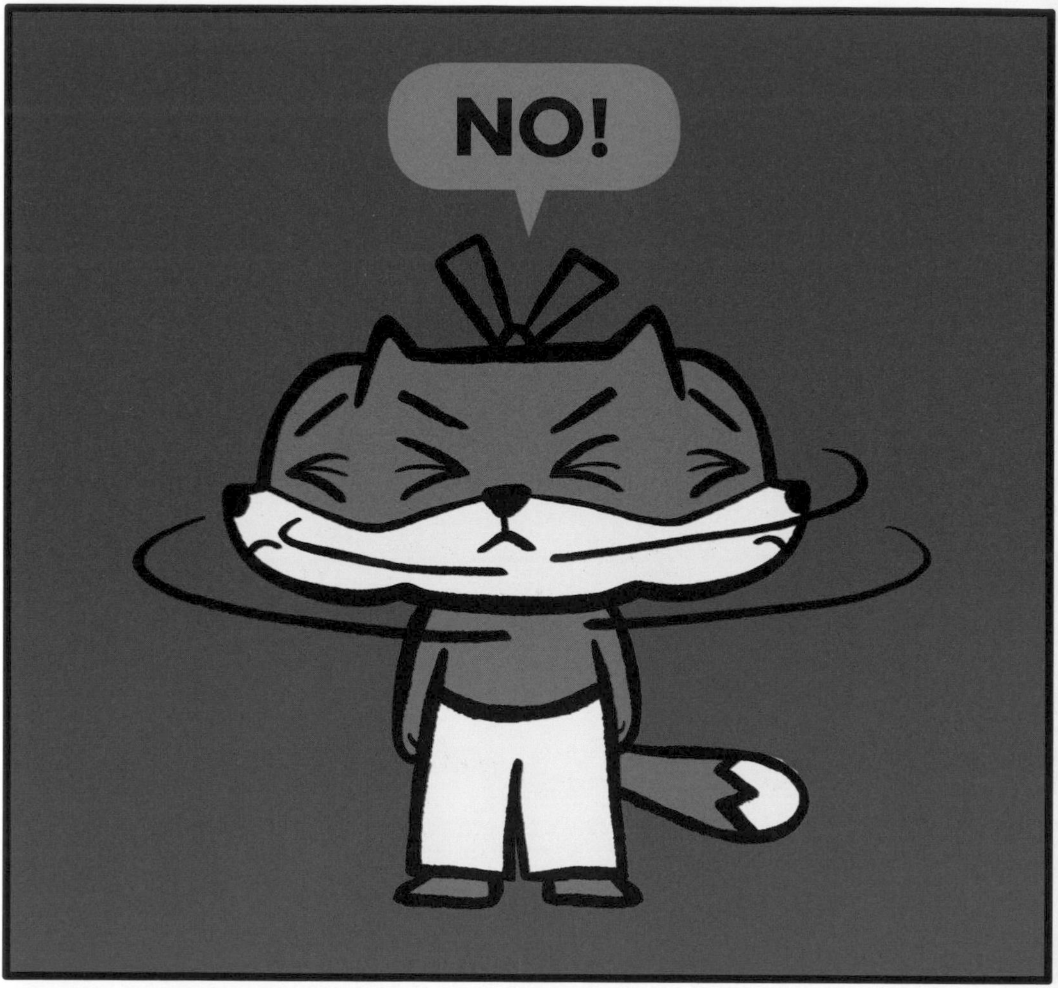
NO!

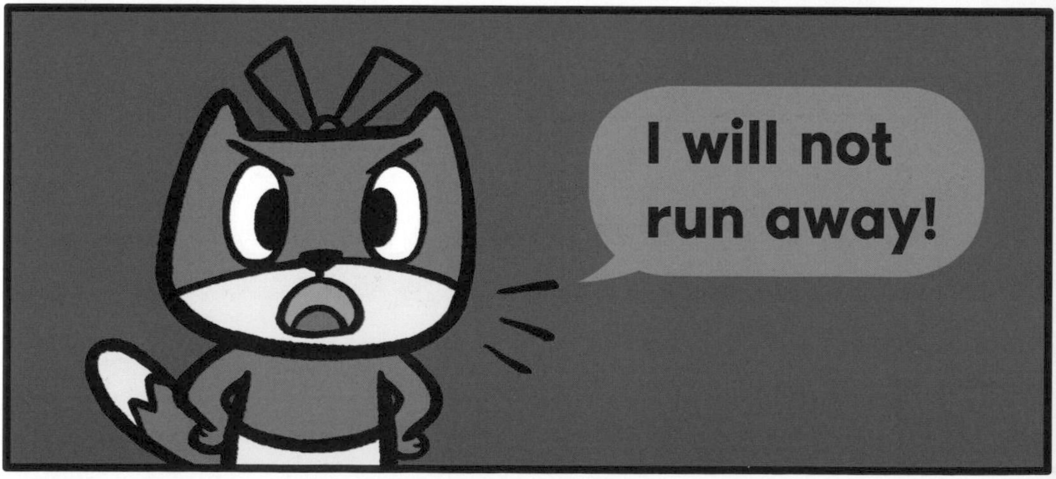
I will not run away!

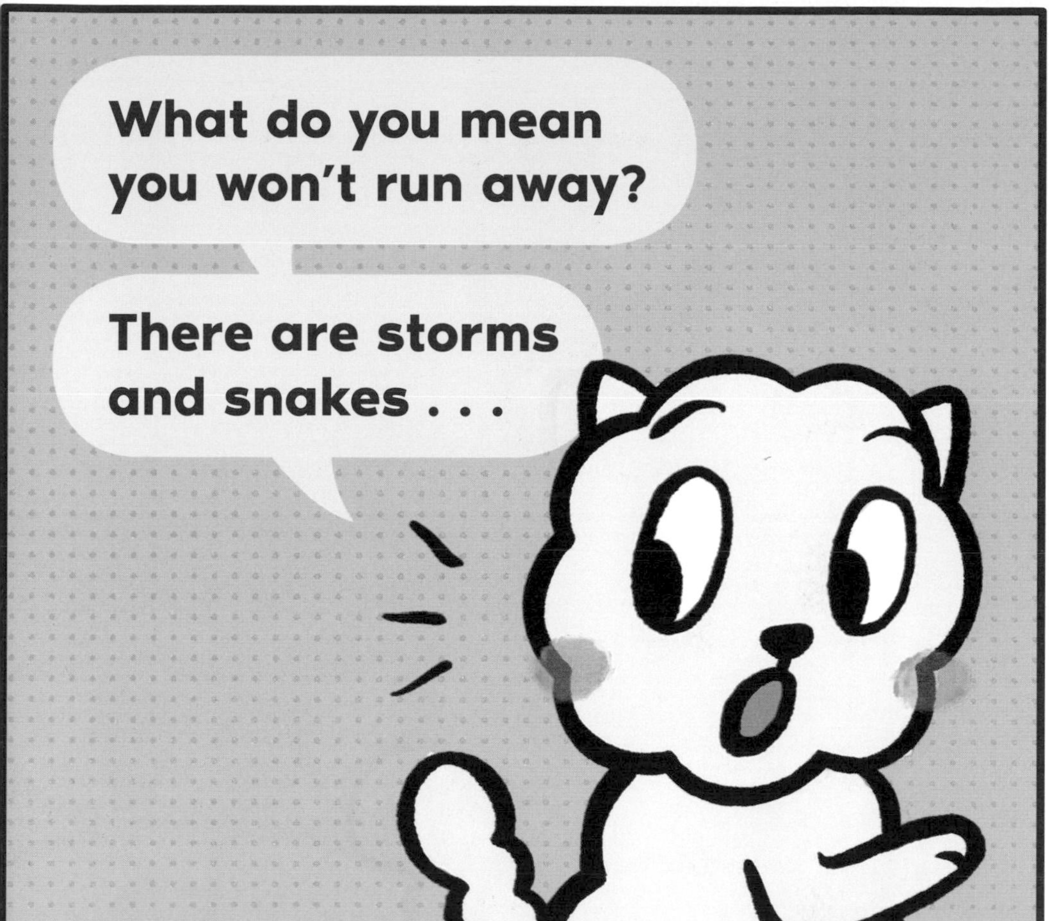
What do you mean you won't run away?
There are storms and snakes . . .

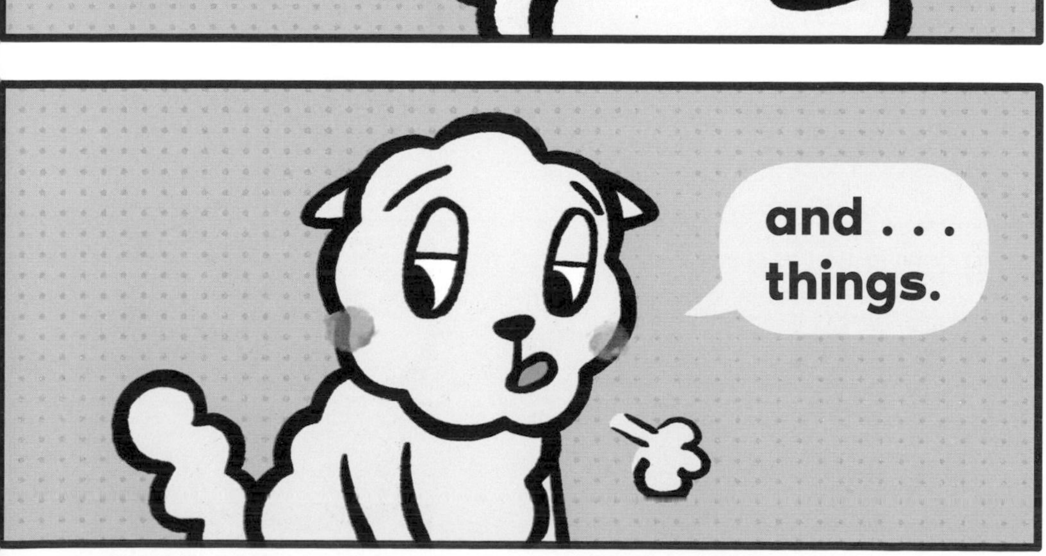
and . . . things.

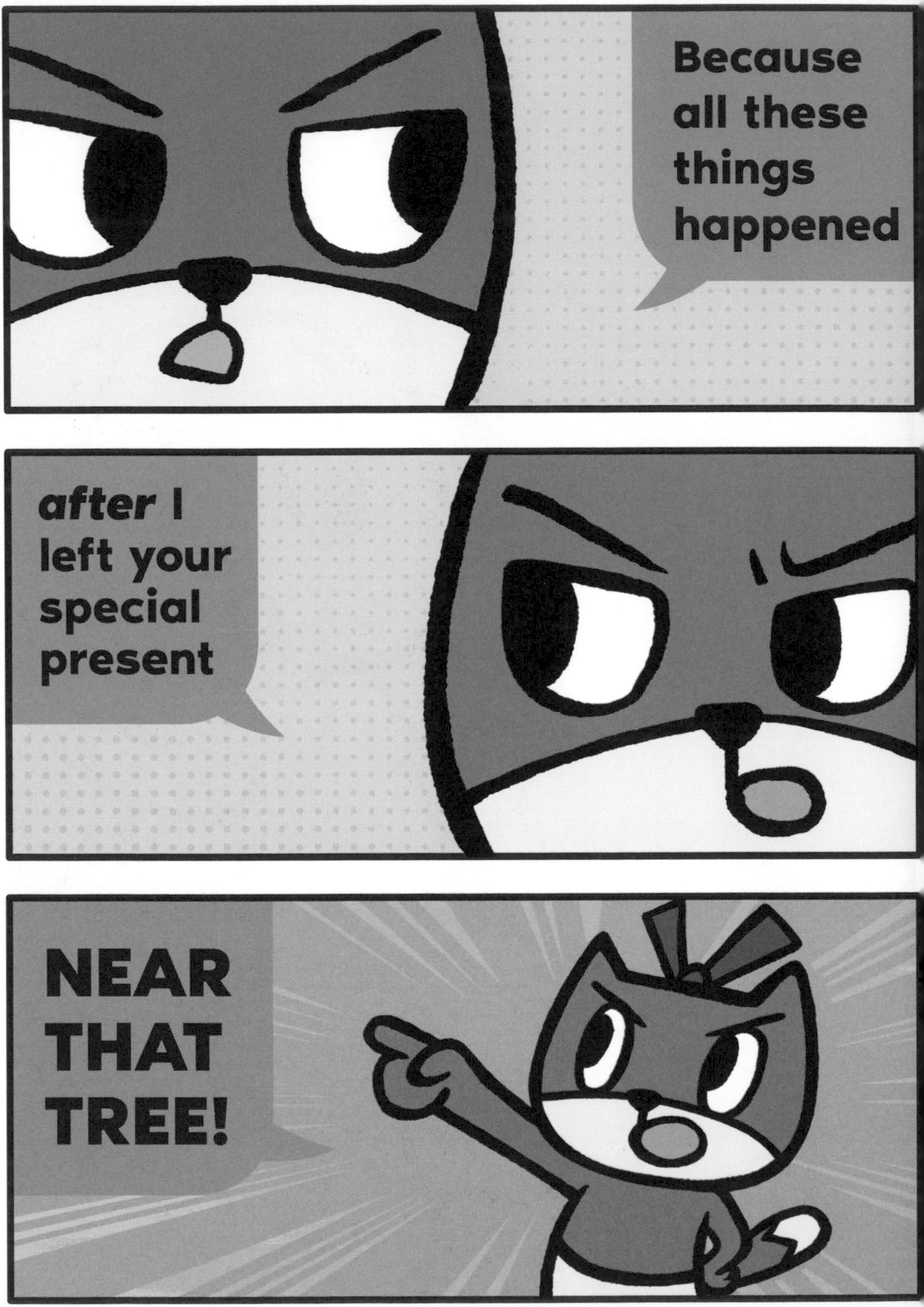
Because all these things happened
after I left your special present
NEAR THAT TREE!

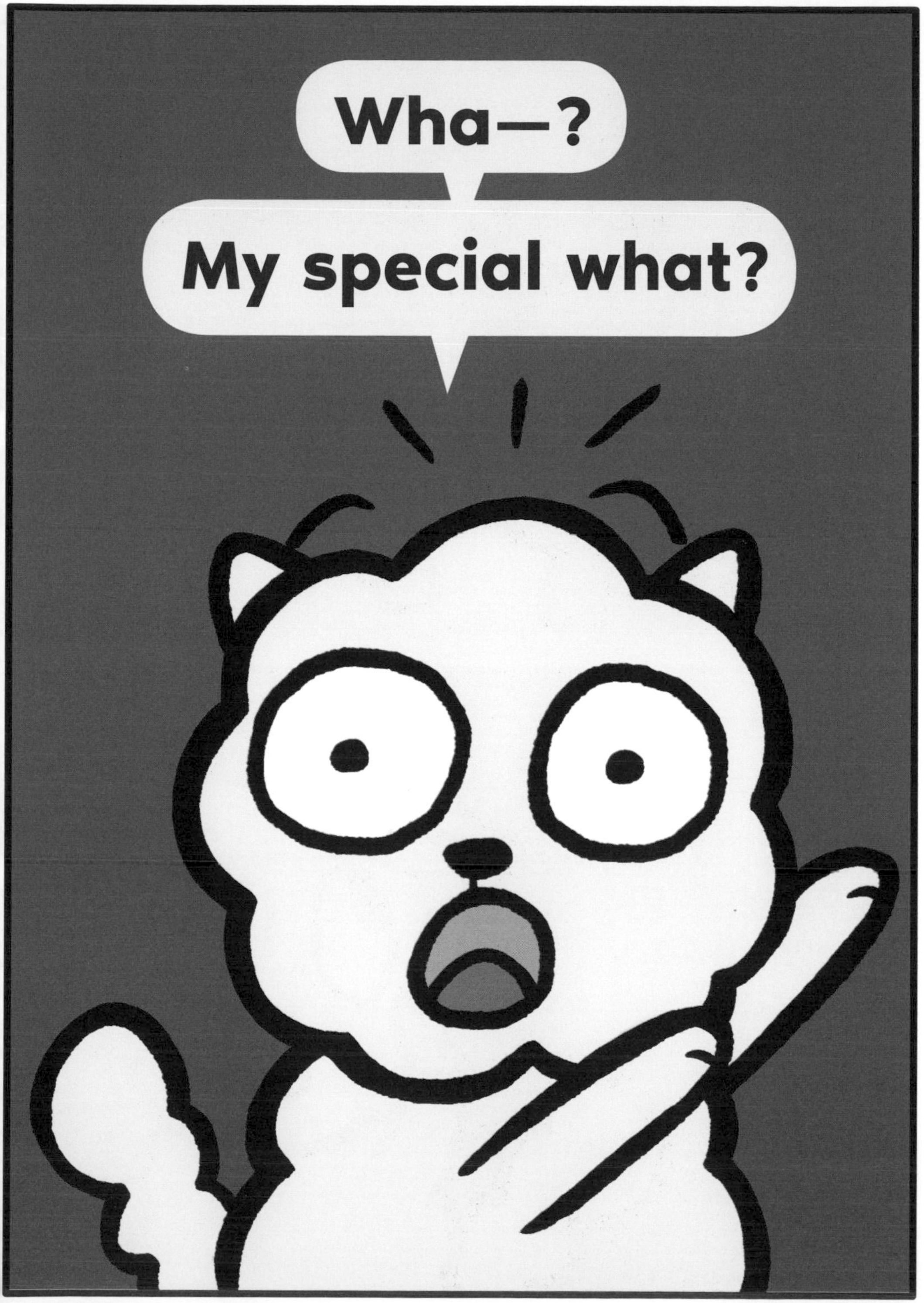
Wha—?
My special what?

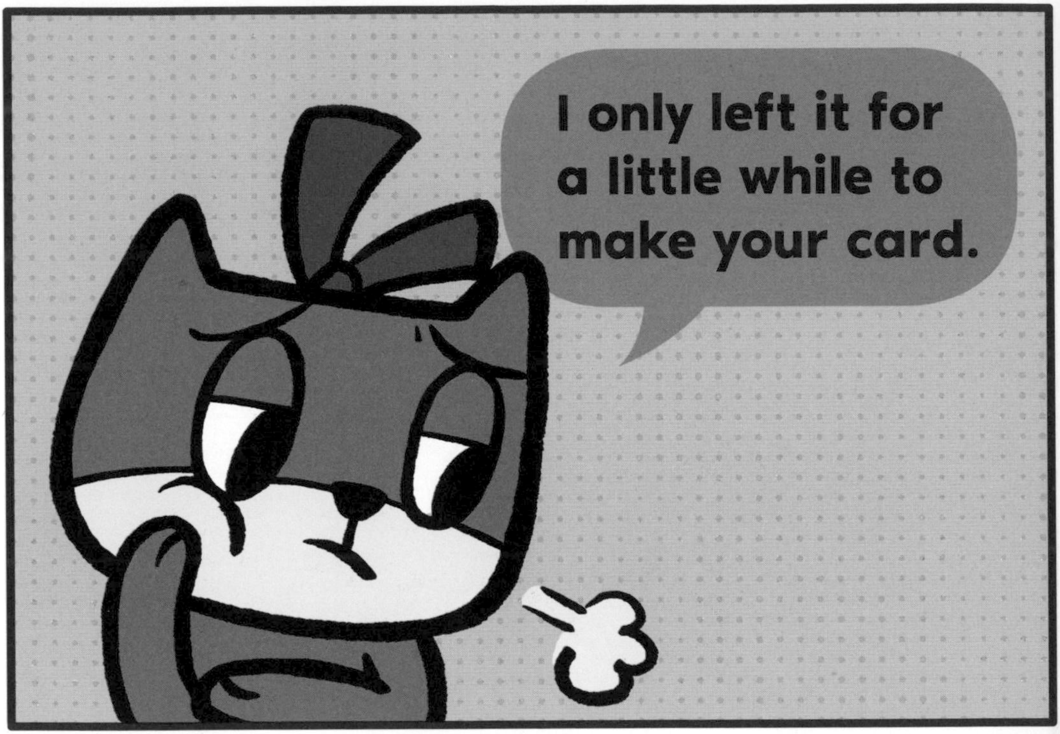
I only left it for a little while to make your card.

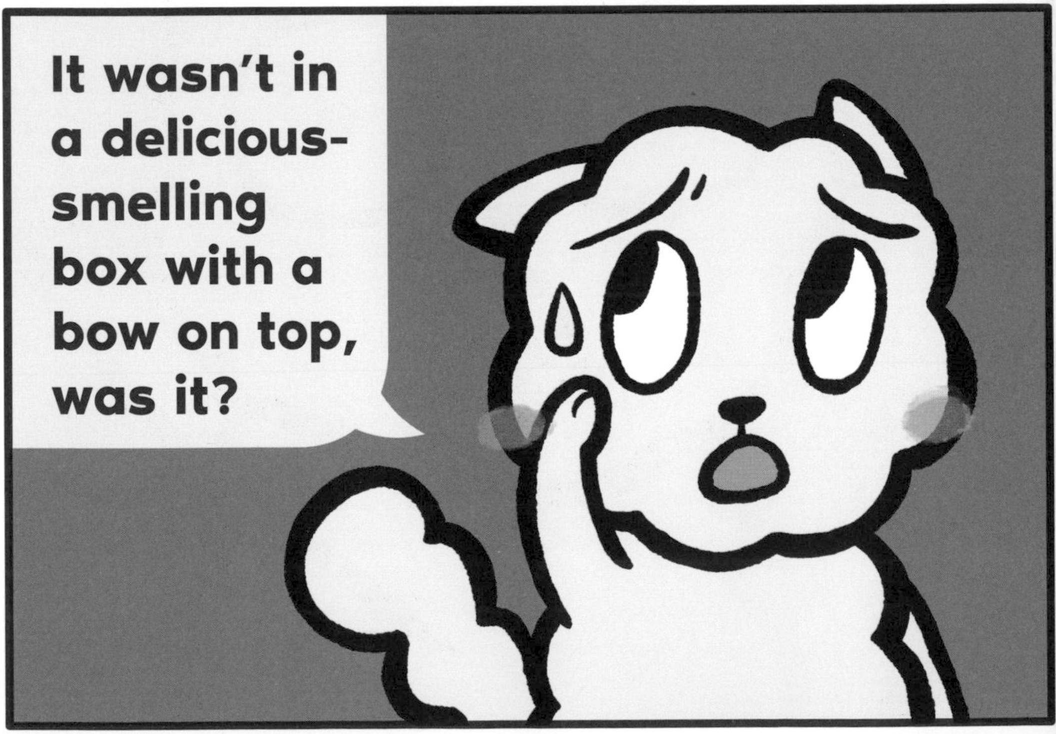
It wasn't in a delicious-smelling box with a bow on top, was it?

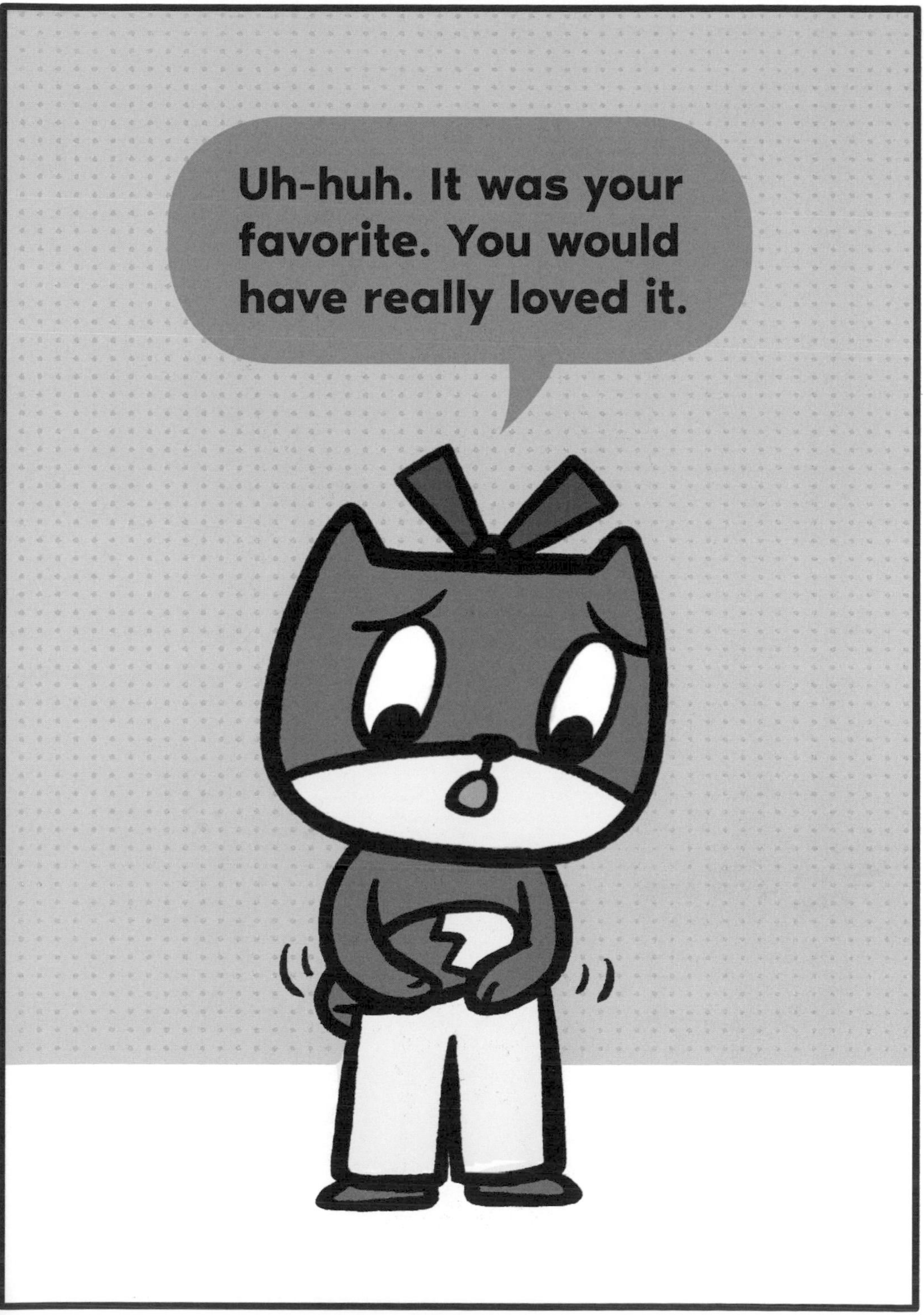
Uh-huh. It was your favorite. You would have really loved it.

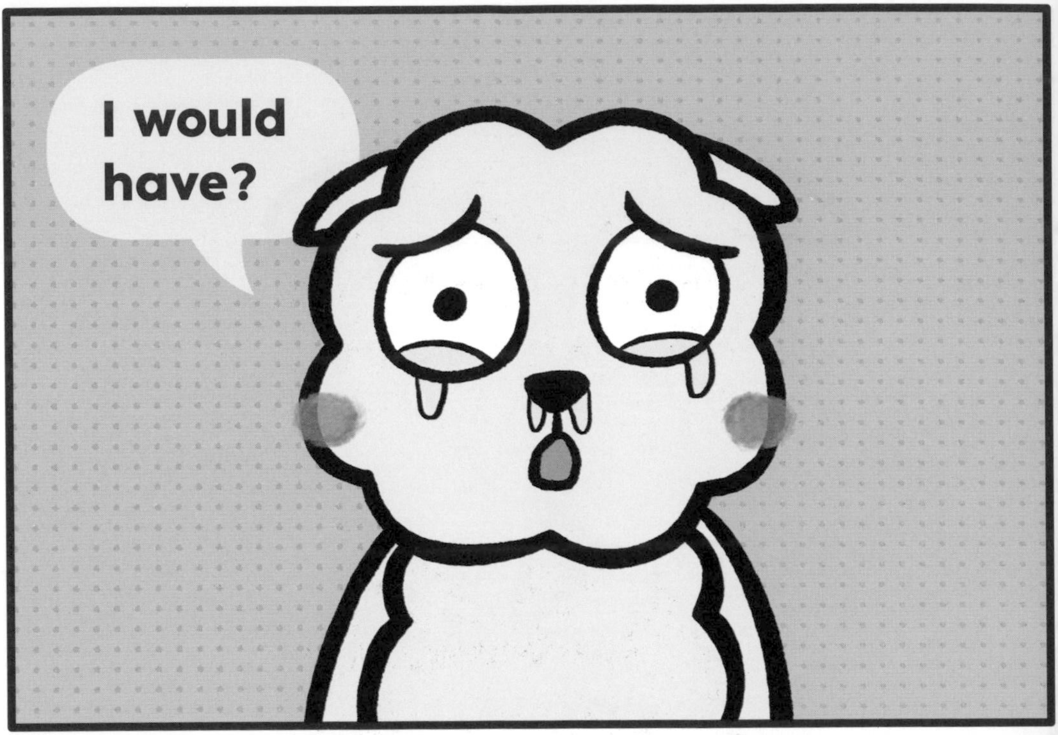
I would have?

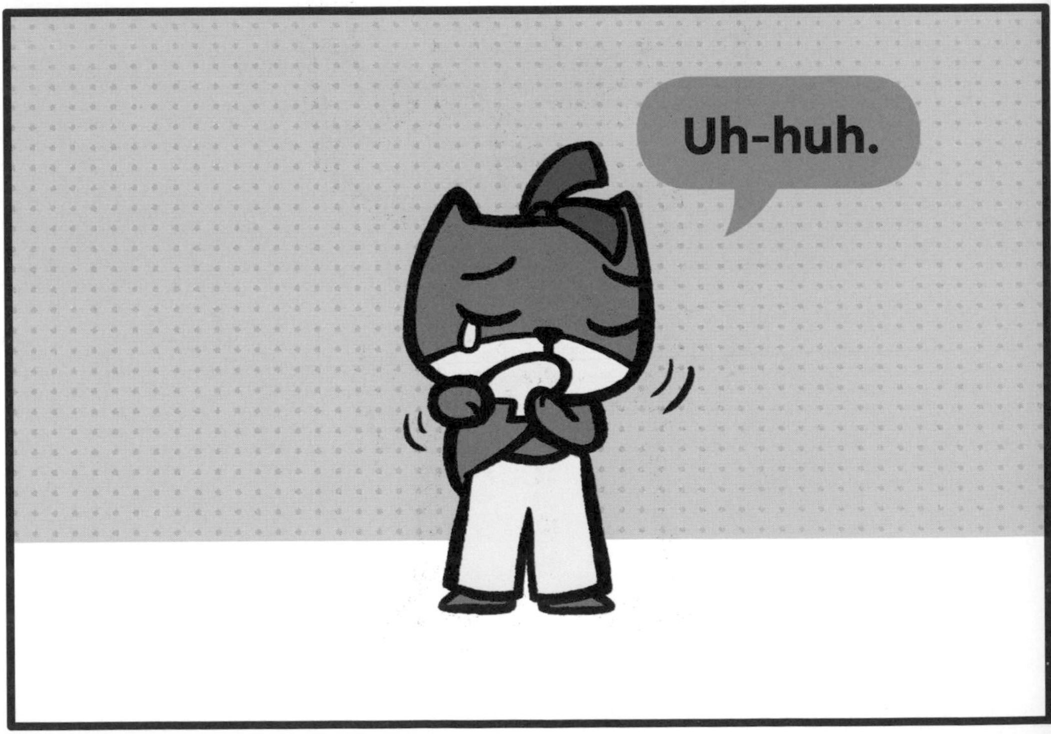
Uh-huh.

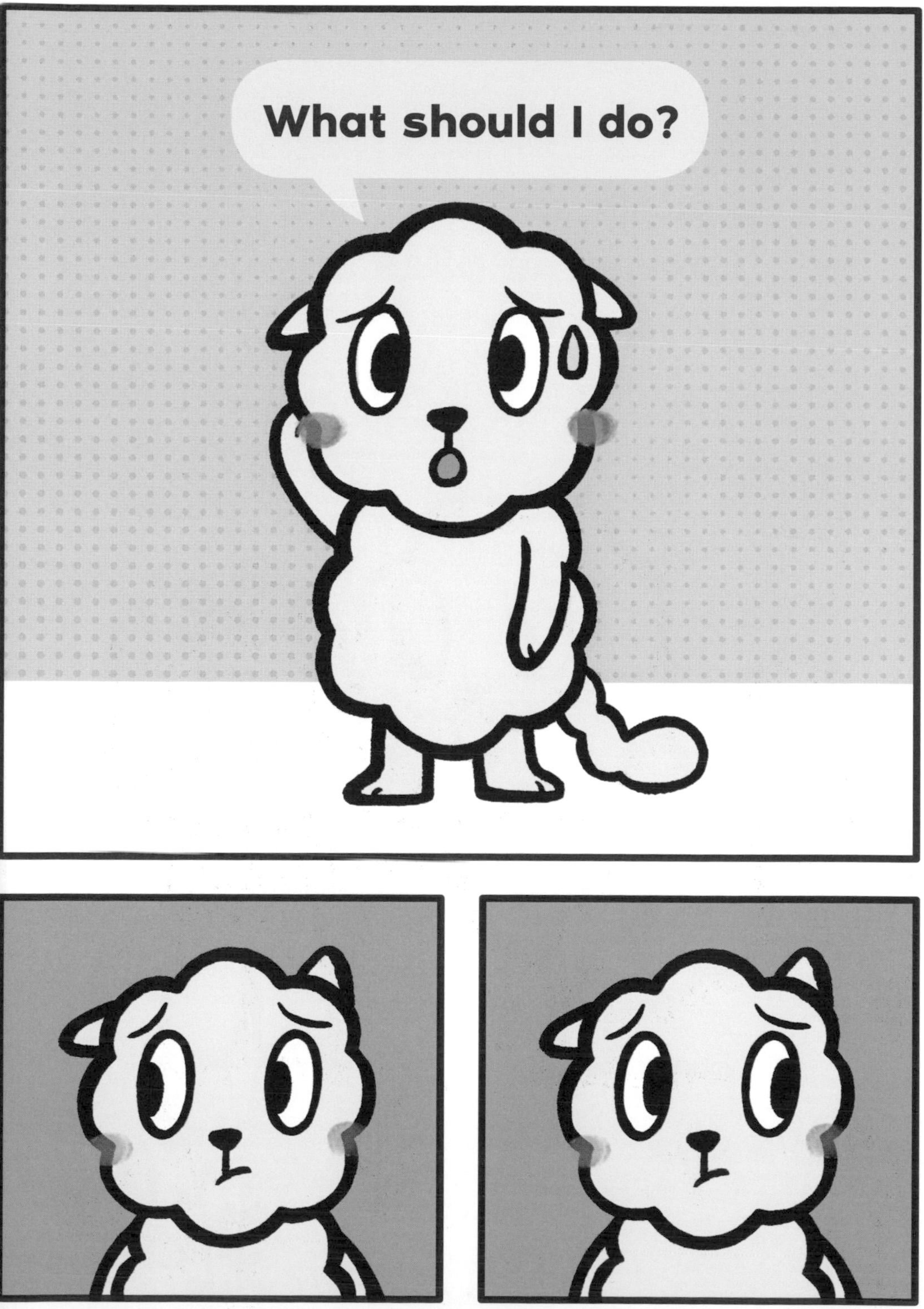
What should I do?

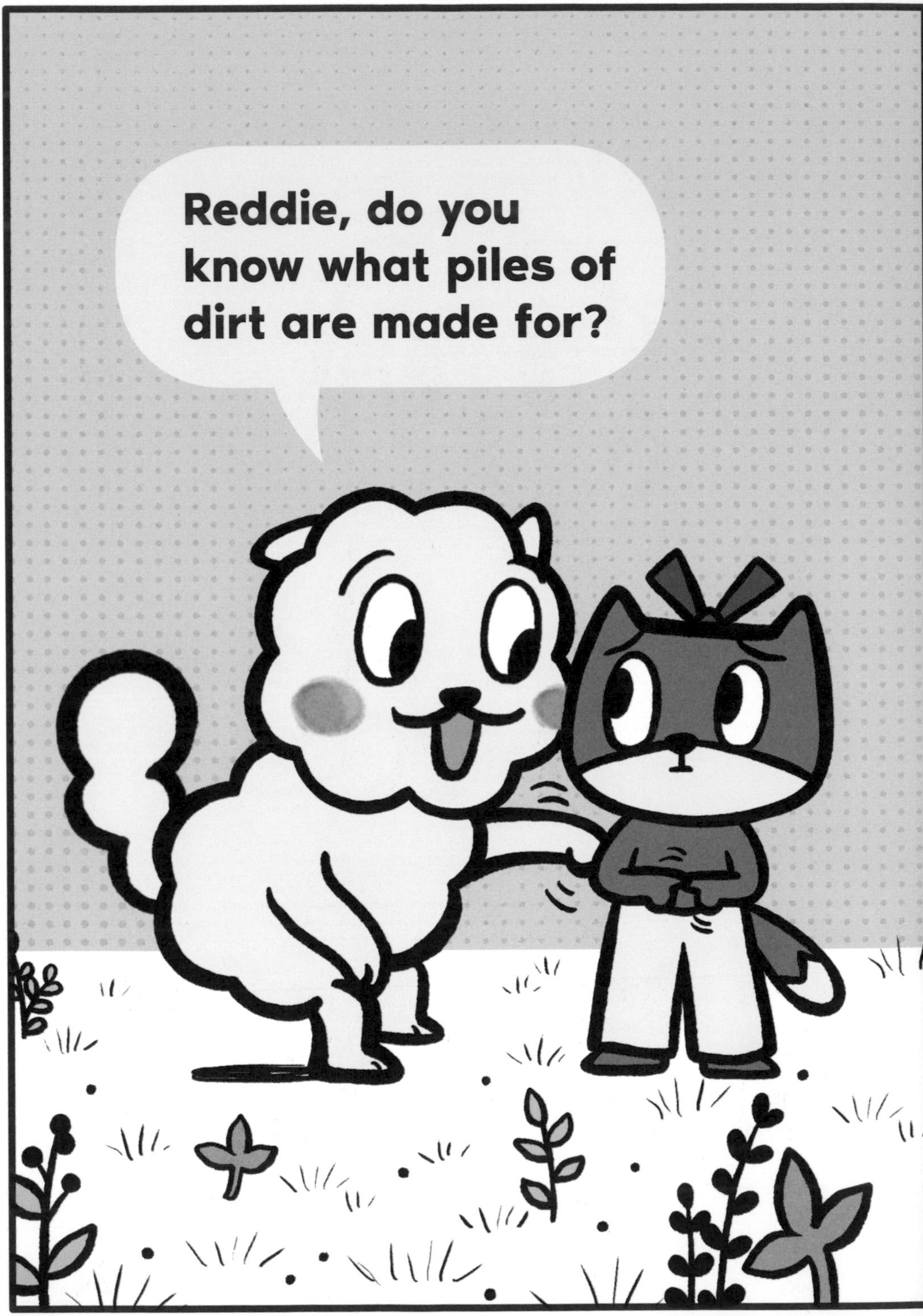
Reddie, do you know what piles of dirt are made for?

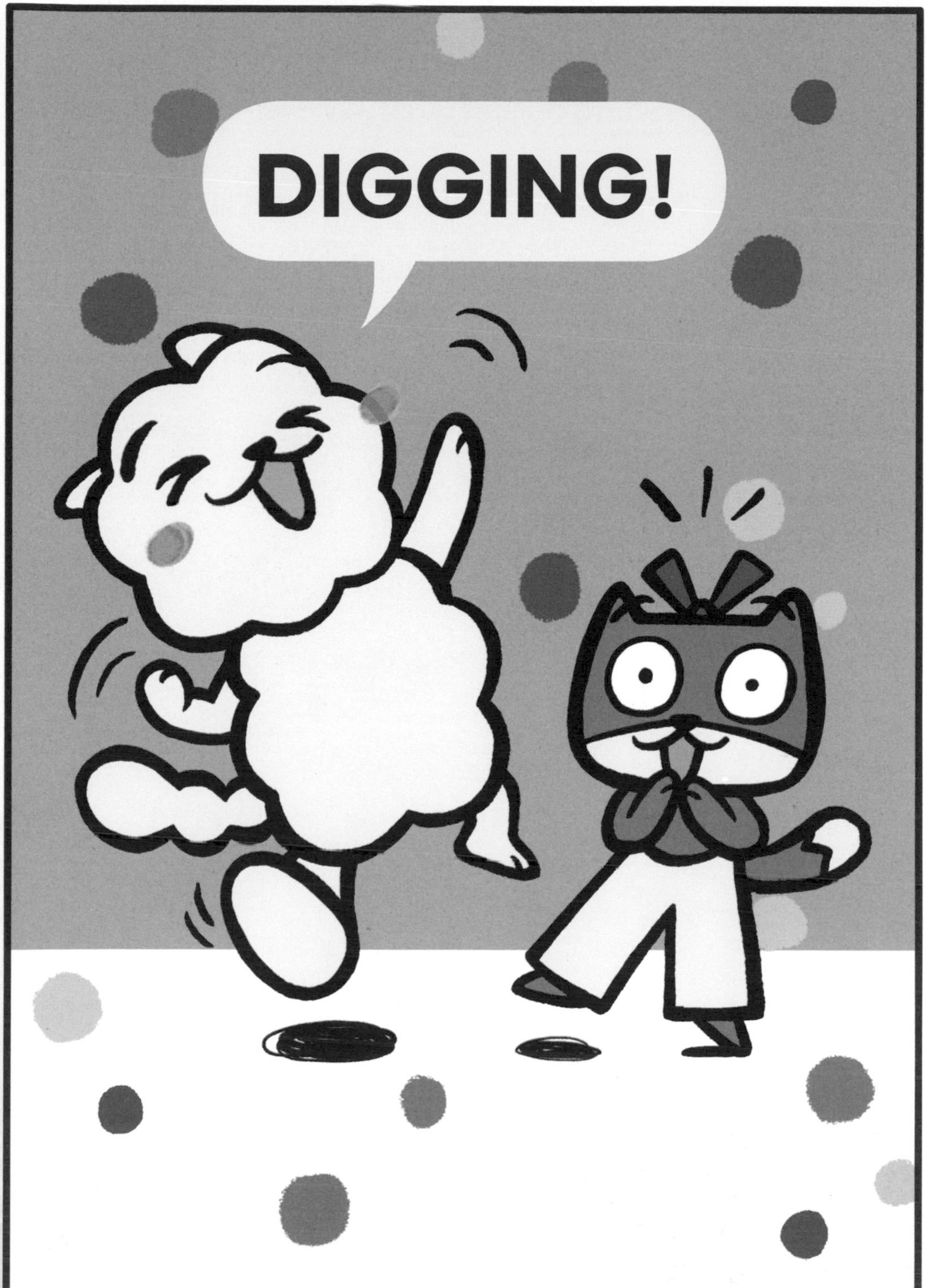
DIGGING!

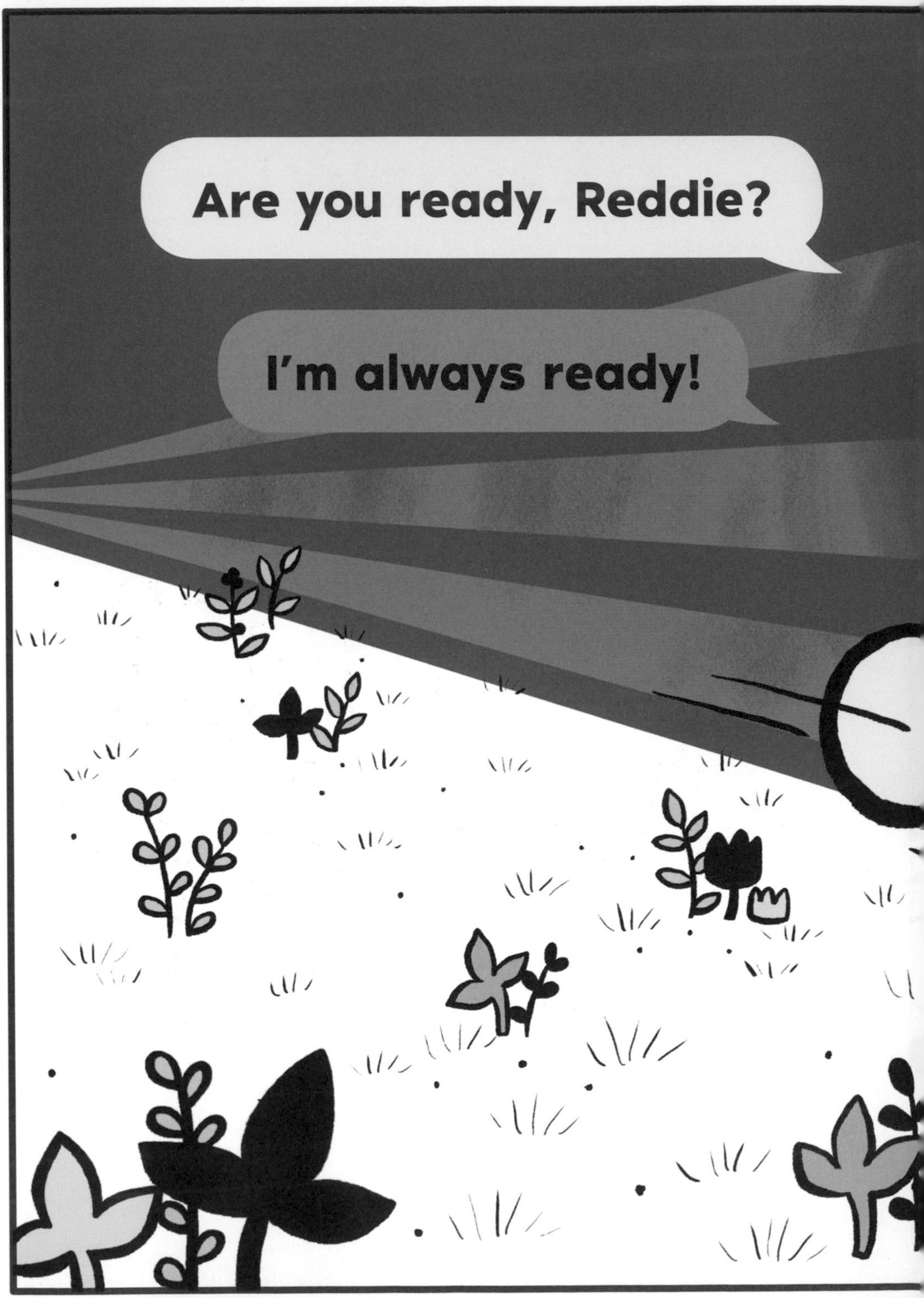
Are you ready, Reddie?
I'm always ready!

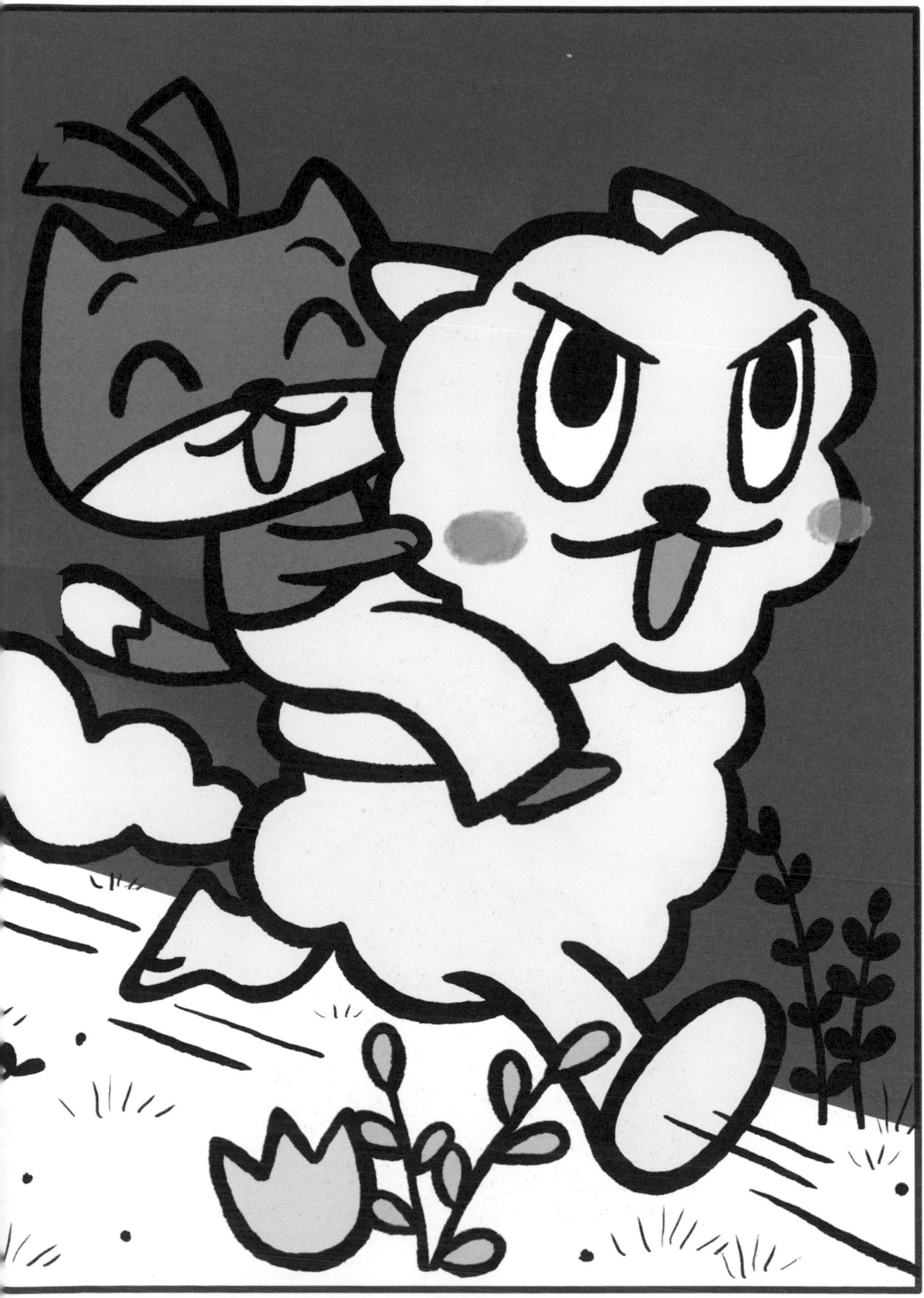

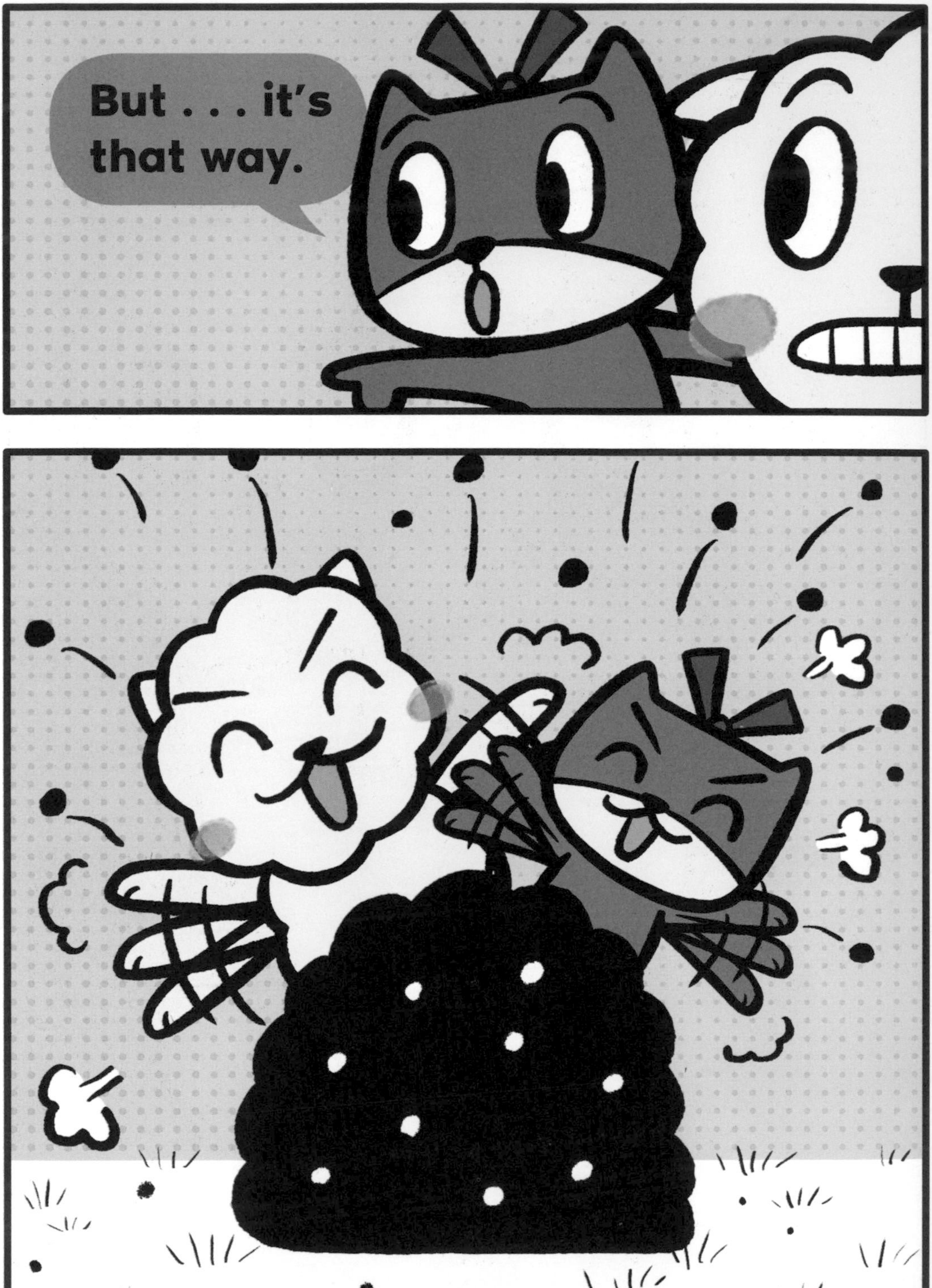
But . . . it's that way.

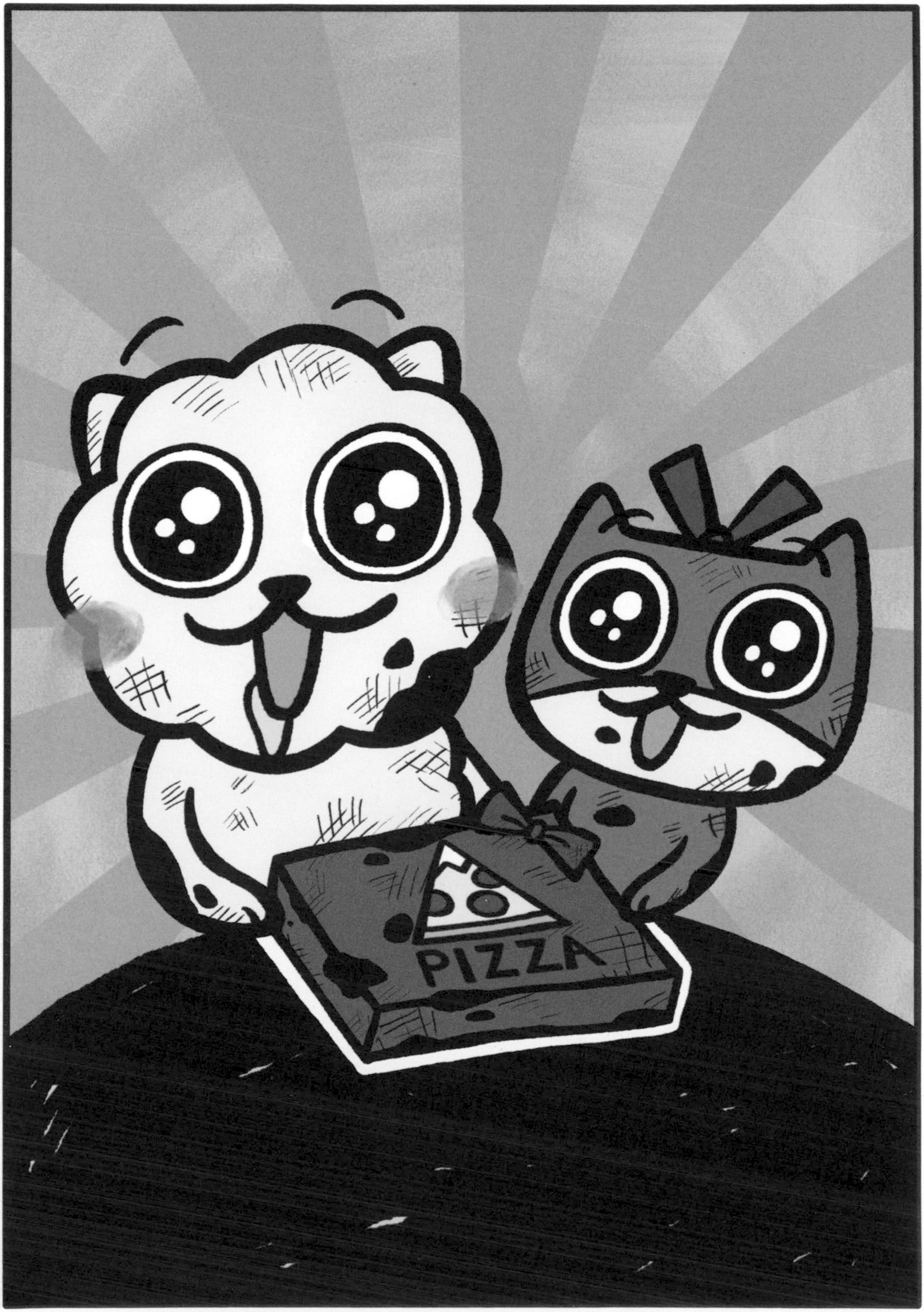
PIZZA

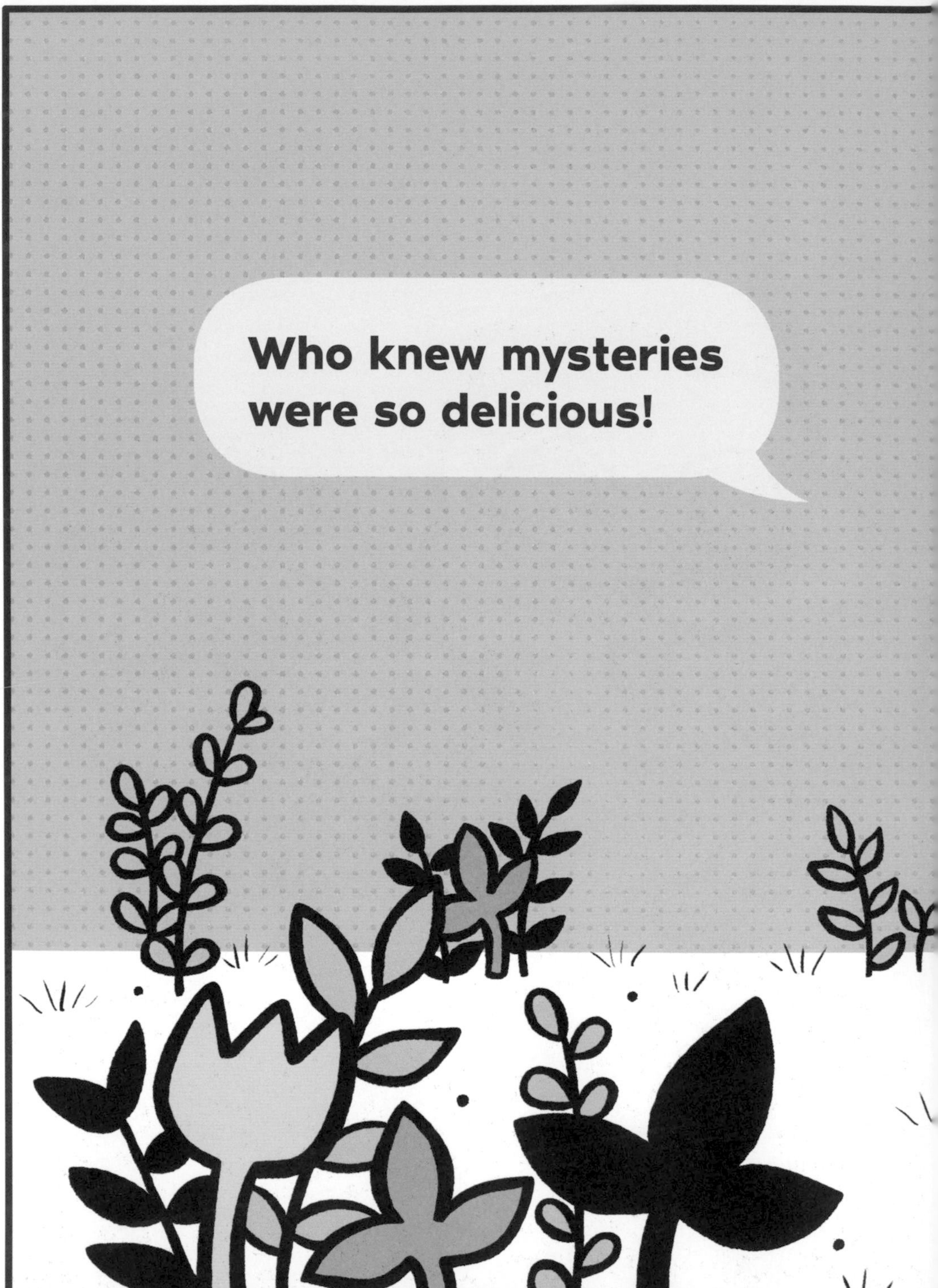
Who knew mysteries were so delicious!

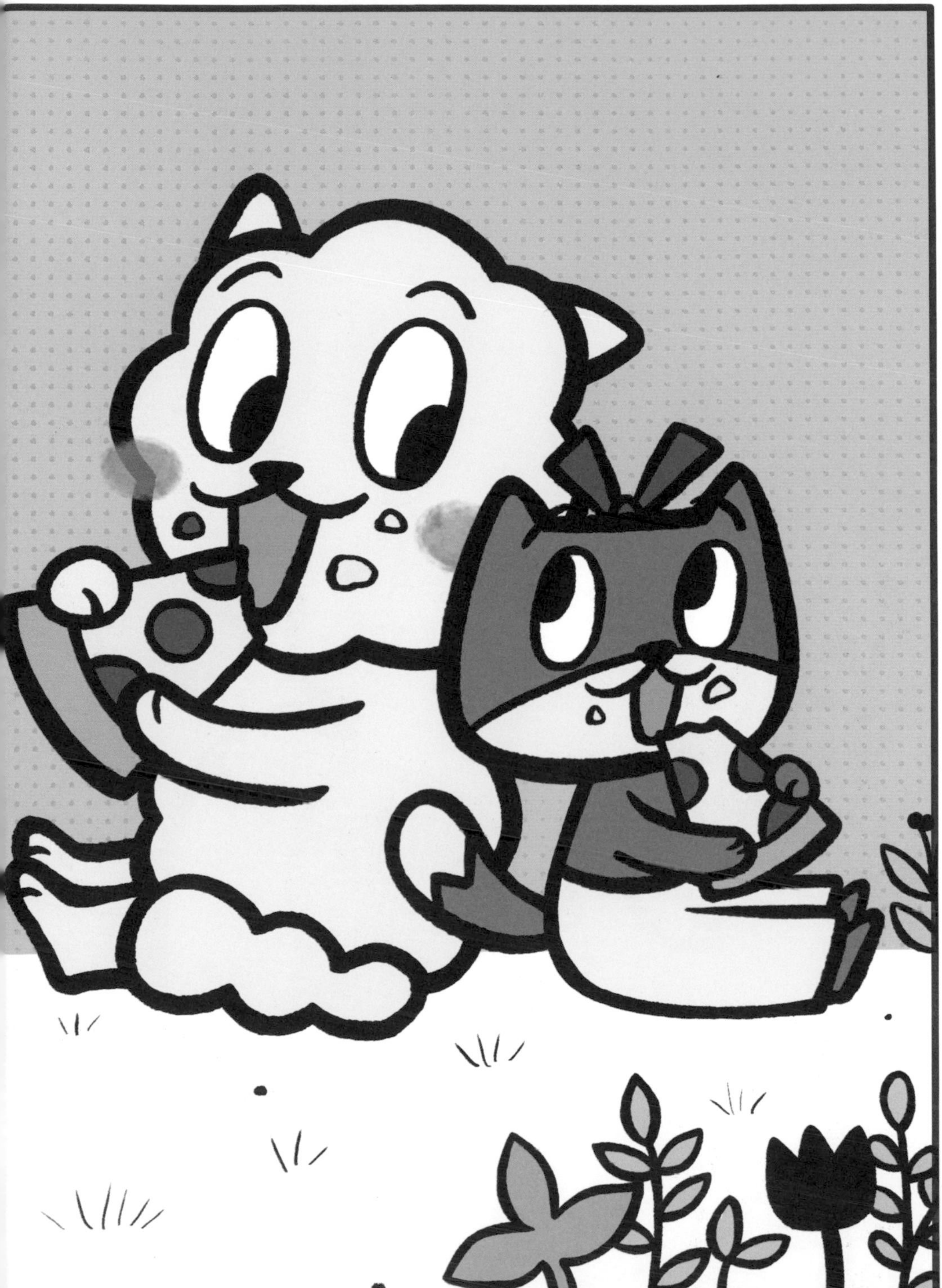

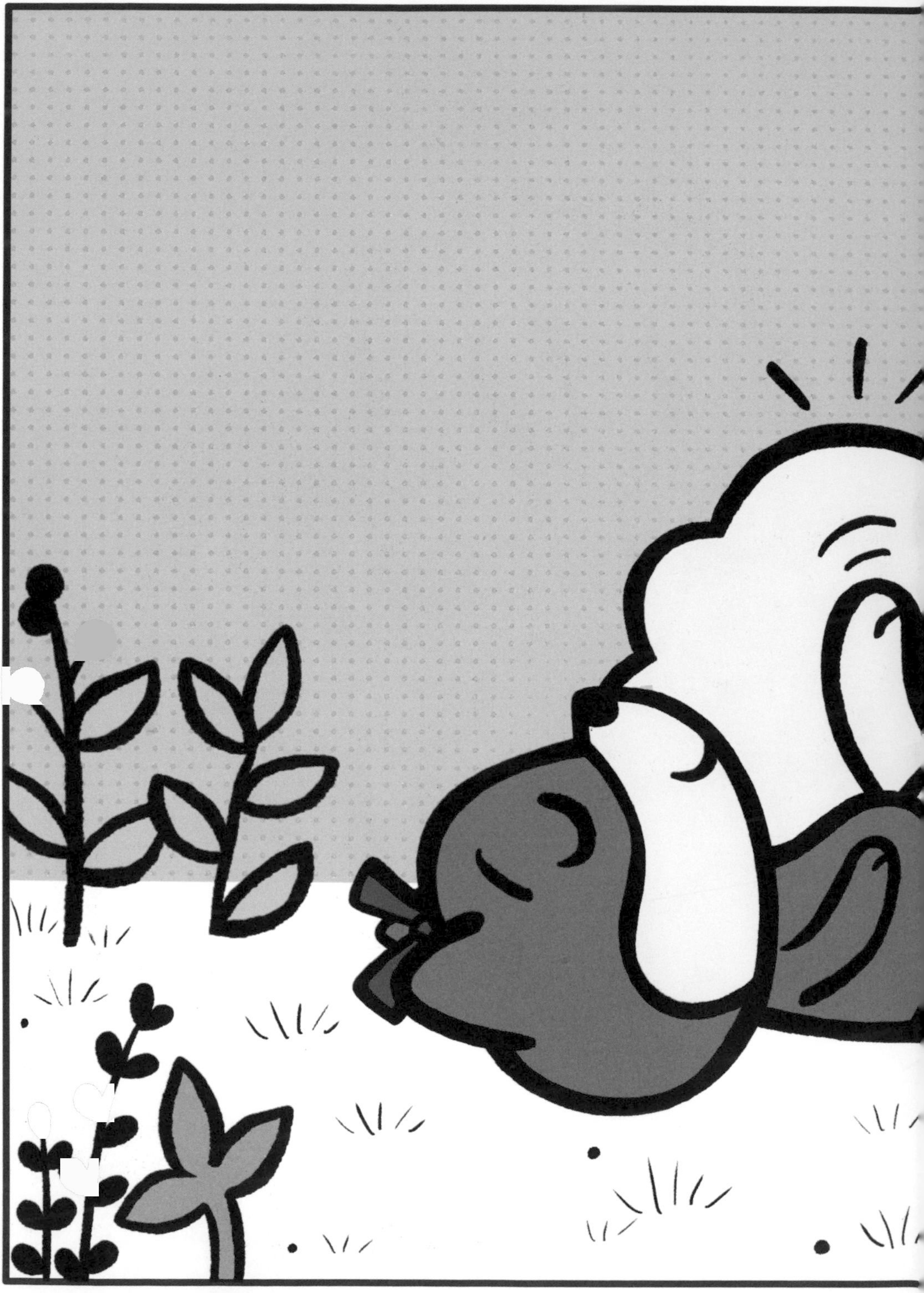

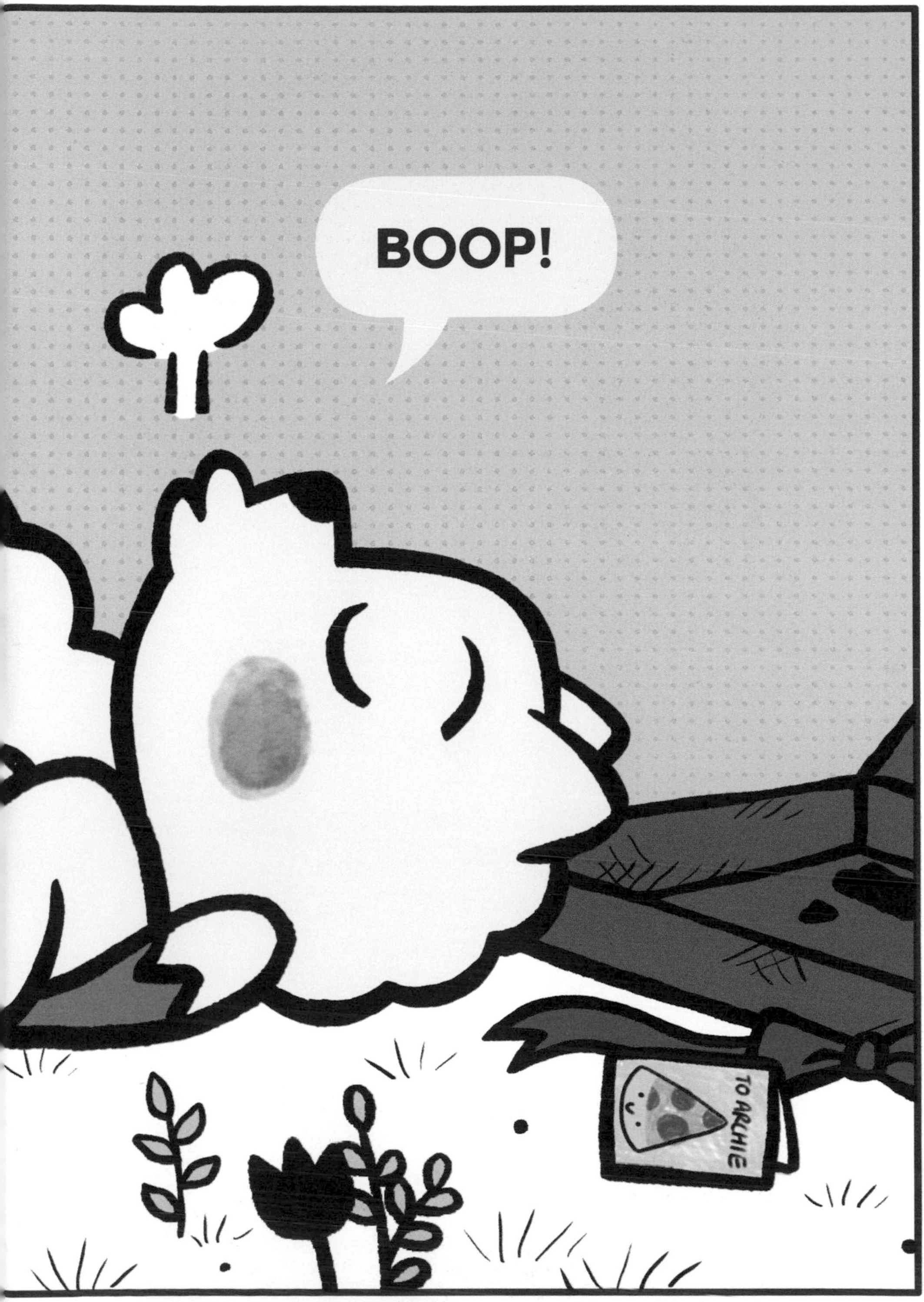
BOOP!
TO ARCHIE

MEET THE MAKERS

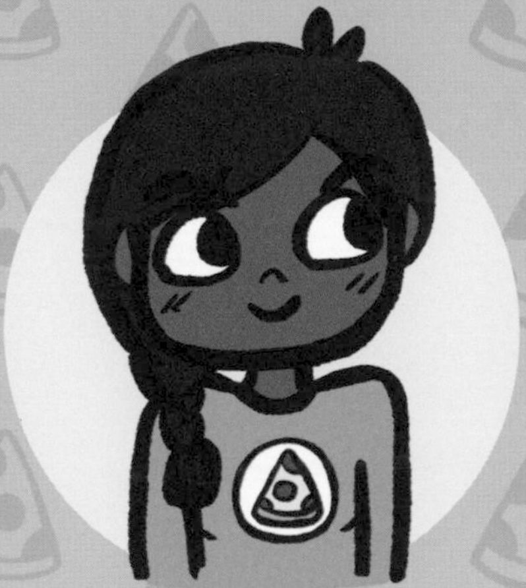

CANDY
draws

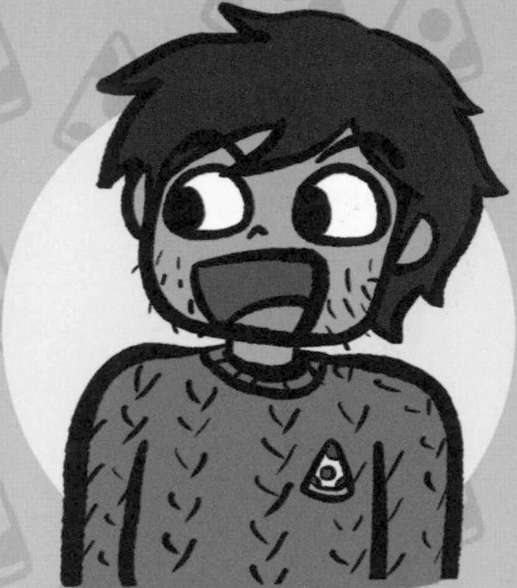

JAMES
writes

Candy James is a husband-and-wife creative duo originally from Hong Kong and New Zealand, but now living on a thickly forested hill in Ballarat, Australia. They are toy, graphic, and garden designers who love to make funny books for children.

What's their favorite pizza topping?

A super-tall mountain of every topping!

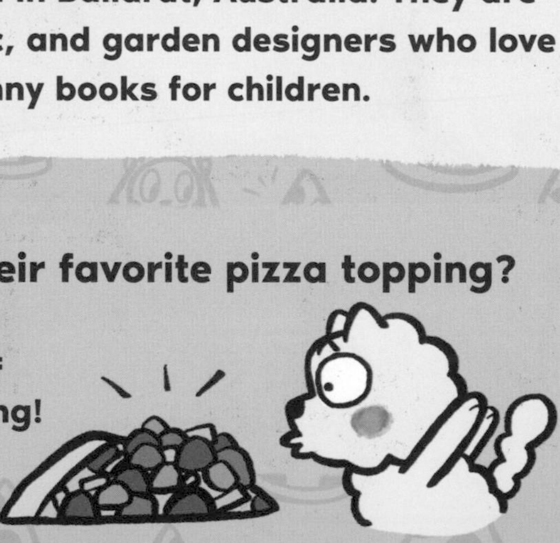